Derek Raymond was born Robin Cook in 1931. His novels include *A State of Denmark, How the Dead Live* and *I Was Dora Suarez*. His most recent book is his autobiography, *The Hidden Files*. He now lives in London.

The Crust
on its Uppers

DEREK RAYMOND

SERPENT'S
TAIL

British Library Cataloguing in Publication Data
Raymond, Derek
  Crust on its Uppers. – New ed. – (Mask Noir series)
  I. Title   II. Series
  823.914[F]

  ISBN 1-85242-268-8

First published by New Authors Limited, an imprint of the
Hutchinson Group, 1962
Copyright © 1962 by Robin Cook

This edition first published by
Serpent's Tail, 4 Blackstock Mews, London N4

Printed in Great Britain by Cox & Wyman Ltd., of Reading, Berkshire

GLOSSARY

In general criminals cut off the final word of rhyming slang phrases, the object being to confuse casual listeners as to their true meaning.

A long one = £1,000
A pony = £25
A score = £20
A ton = £100 (half a ton = £50)
Angst = trouble
Archbishop = Archbishop Laud = fraud

Baize, the = Bayswater Road
Barnet = barnet fair = hair
Beehive = five = £5
Bin = pocket
Binns = spectacles (dark binns = dark glasses)
Blag = a bluff, a tall story (Fr. '*blague*'?) Also as verb
Boat = boat-race = face
Boiler = a well-used woman of forty or over
Bottle = bottle-and-glass = arse
Bristols = bristol cities = well, mammary glands
Broads = playing cards
Bubble = bubble-and-squeak = Greek (thus Archbubble = Archgreek or Greek-in-chief)

Camp about, to = to pirouette and gesture eloquently
Carpet = twelve months' jail
Cat's-meat gaff = hospital

Charver = to have sex with
Chat someone up, to = see 'blag'
Cobblers = cobbler's awls = balls
Cock-and-hen = ten = £10
Cop for = to pick up, i.e. telephone

Dabs = fingerprints
Deviator = a crook (devious = crooked; deviation = a crime)
Dinge = a negro
Do bird, to = to go to prison
Dot-and-dash = cash
Drum = room or flat
Duke = duke of kent = rent
Dummy = a deaf-mute

Exes = expenses

Flash = front
Form = a prison record
44X = extreme, i.e. '44X angst' = big trouble

Gaff = living quarters
g.b.h. = grievous bodily harm
Grand = thousand

Half a bar = ten shillings
Hampsteads = hampstead heath = teeth

Have it away on the hurry-up, have it away on your toes = to leave a place smartly

Have it away with something = to steal

Have it off with, to = to have sex with someone

Have someone well under the cosh = have someone just where you want them

Have the (dead) needle, to = to be (very) angry with someone

Horsed = condition after taking heroin

Ice-cream = ice-cream freezer = geezer

In the death = in the end

Jack-and-jill = the bill

Jamjar = car (also 'jam')

John = a john bull = a pull = an arrest

Keep the obbs on someone, to = keep someone under observation

Kettle = wristwatch

Kick = pocket

Kite = a cheque ('kiting-book'= cheque-book: 'fly a dodgy kite' = write a bad cheque)

Knock, to = get an article or meal on credit and not pay, or pay by bad cheque

Knocking company = hire-purchase company

Kosher = smart, good, all right, not 'bent', etc., according to context

Lamp, to = to look

Lifters = hands

Linen = linen-draper = newspaper

Manor = the area where one lives and is known

Marching money = small change to get from place A to B

Mark someone's card, to = give someone a tip or information

Minces = mince-pies = eyes

Moisher, to = to wander

Monkey = £500

Moody, to = to persuade someone you hold cards you in fact don't; to bluff; hence a conman's 'story', 'blag' or 'chat' or any 'devious' proposition is described as 'moody' (also as noun and adjective)

Morrie = reverse of Slag

Nishte = nothing

Nosh, to = to eat (also as noun meaning 'meal')

Old, the = money owing from before (usually from cards or racing)

Old Bill (or Uncle Bill) = the police

Pull a stroke = to be faster, smarter, quicker than your opponent

Punter = here not quite as in racing, but more, someone with money looking for a scheme to put it into and ignorant of the ways of the morrie world. An extreme case would be called 'a mug punter' or 'a half-wide mug'

Rabbit, to = to talk, chat (also as noun)

Reddy, reddies = cash

River ooze = booze (more often simply 'the river')

Scotches = scotch pegs = legs
Screw = a prison warder
Scrubber = unwashed female teenager
Shickered = broke
Shiv, to = to cut someone's face with a razor (also as noun)
Six-and-eight = straight
Slag = young third-rate grafters, male or female, unwashed, useless
Slush = counterfeit money
Snap = ampoules of amyl nitrate sewn into cotton-wool pads. They are broken with a sharp sound under the nose and inhaled, whence 'snap'
Snout = cigarette
Snout baron = Prisoner with outside source of tobacco who makes money trading it with the less fortunate
Spieler = place where cards, chemmy, poker, etc., are played
Stay stumm, to = keep silent

Stubs = teeth
Sus, to = to suspect (also as noun and even adjective)
Sweeper on the twos = prisoner whose job it is to sweep the second floor of the jail

Tealeaf = a thief
Ten-stretch = ten years in jail
Three-handed = a gang of three (also two-handed, mob-handed, etc.)
Tomfoolery = jewellery
Topped = lit. have one's top cut off; hence, to be killed or executed
Trout, be all about = to be on the *qui vive*
Twenty-two carat = absolutely trustworthy
Twirl = a key

Vera = vera lynn = gin
ville, the = Pentonville Prison

X (pronounced 'ex') = cross, annoyed

FOREWORD

THEY SAY I've got three hundred and fifty words to tell you why I'm in print. This is no blag, then, morrie. It's a tale of someone who wanted to go and *go*—who was sick of the dead-on-its-feet upper crust he was born into, that he didn't believe in, didn't want, whose values were meaningless, that did nothing but hold him back from his first nanny onwards. I wanted to chip my way out of that background which held me like a flea in a block of ice, and crime was the only chisel I could find.

People in that world are vivid, whatever else. They're British, too, as you'll immediately see; only, any phlegm they may have had they've coughed up long ago in the hope it's a gold watch with handles.

The other two morries you'll meet are the same as me, same background, same drives—and you'll read how, driven by a savage, subconscious desire to smash up and revolt against a clique that no longer means anything we wanted to say, we all three worked for the communists to the tune of a quarter of a million quid and nearly got away with it.

Not quite, though.

You may think, when you've read this, that we're just a trio of cynical hoods who ought to have known better, that we got everything we had coming, that jail's maybe the best place for us. So we are. So we did. So perhaps it is.

We know how you all love to shiver and say 'Ooh!' and camp about at the mention of the word 'crime'. Okay. This is the red meat of a *crime*, so read it and then curl up in your feather bed and forget it. That's fine. *You* never pushed all your chips out beyond the white line. So you've no winnings to collect and you've nothing to pay either.

But we have. We've exchanged the Sèvres china in our ancestral homes for something not nearly so nice. Two of us have years in jail to figure out the meaning of what we did. The third has eternity.

Any *glamour* this book has is the glamour that surrounds people who giggle when they're squeezed into a little box of existence where one side's a diminishing chance of survival and the other three are time running out. Maybe, too, glamour always surrounds a loser.

That's one thing we were taught to do really well.

THE CRUST ON ITS UPPERS

★

I

I MUST warn you that everything that follows emanates from the following figure: sacked from the most super public school in the country at the age of sixteen. Puzzled. Sacked from crammer the following year, with clap caught from the Greek maid. Still puzzled. Joined the army because still too green to knock. Glowing career at Mons, blinded by the toothpaste smile reflected from my boots at adjutant's parade? Certainly not. Latrines corporal. Still puzzled. Illegitimate child in Weymouth, now about nine—one of the few things that made sense in those days, because the punishment fitted the crime: Daisy was a right old boiler. Demobbed with the following report: Officer potential, nil—N.C.O. potential, nil. C.O.'s comment: a very poor soldier indeed, with a nice smile. What next? Oxford and turn over a new leaf? No, no, morrie, I was beginning to learn . . . to the north, full of demon energy: to London—a proper ice-cream to look at, only I assure you I'm all about trout, aged twenty-eight with a hard apprenticeship behind me since those army days: two years in Spain flogging hot tape-recorders, a year in France busy vanishing; I lived on the Left Bank subsisting on ten poundses my mother sent me in *Illustrated London Newses*, taking Civilization at the Sorbonne and penicillin for clap, living all that year like a sort of Lucifer among the scabs and crabs, with a record player roaring out skiffle and trad jazz on the end of the bed. Odd period in London—but come to a rub: nishte. Then off to Rome where I had a right touch teaching at a languages school; nipped off on the plane with Anzac Jack, a dead young grafter, leaving a whole load of angst behind. Anzac played it cool out there: I believe he still is —in New York, married to a watches heiress and fooling them all on Madison Avenue. Anyway, having copped on to this job in London and been flown out by the old darling who ran the joint, at first it was dead boring, playing the half-wide mug on ten bob an hour; but we soon got organized and grafted four ton apiece from the old dear and got to the States. Looking back I've done some odd things, but all down to learning; I've done the lot, in a way, from tutoring a British commercial attaché's son in Latin and Greek to moody rabbits in Spanish bars with my heart going like an outboard motor and my eyes running about in my head like ball-bearings, with plain-clothes Seguridad watching me and a stack of those dodgy tape-recorders outside in the motor. As to form, though, nothing, though that isn't to say that ripples don't pass over the ganglia of the boys down at Chelsea nick every time they clock my boat. And that's not just down to experience, me not having done any bird—just a weird sort of instinct which tells you when enough's enough. My old man? Well he's a *sort* of dustman, as you'll see.

And what do ice-creams like us add up to? Ah, well, that's a question I've often asked myself and the rest of the morries. But nishte. If I knew the answer I daresay I'd be laughing. We all would. 'I can give you the facts,' I'd say, like a super Lord Morrie dictating from his seat in a 707, 'but you'll have to draw the conclusion yourselves.' All I know is I'm a modern, mixed-up, metamorphosed phenomenon, like the other morries, and maybe something'll come out from what's to follow, though I don't know, because I don't know what's to follow myself. As for the other two morries, I was at school with one of them— another point in this strange new world of 1962: there are still only two good schools to come from—and you can guess which *they* are. All the best Anglo-Saxon grafters come from mine, and the Bubbles and the Indians from the other—what you might call the creme of the ice-creme. All the rest of the so-called kosher establishments are really down to the snob angle, trying to moody through to the royal enclosure on the knock, like the slag in the King's Road. The point to grasp is that if your'e a *morrie* you really sit up there. You plan. *If* you live near the King's Road it's just a nasty coincidence. Nothing to boast about. You know how you hear the slag in the Cavalryman rabbiting about the morries pub, the Tealeaf up in Park Lane—Lord This and Morrie That—well, that's how the slag gives itself away. The real morries never do that. Don't have to, do they? They're all about trout, flying dodgy kites with each other at bent spielers till the punter, for very shame, outs his kiting-book too and scribbles a straight one, sort of not to be outdone. And even when the old firm's going a bit unsteady morries never hock their gold kettles and *never* walk or bus it like the slag do. *Always* the XK or the three-point-four, *never* the Sprite or the knocker's aged small-boot Bentley or the A30 van.

Now for a quick lamp over the slag. Ever had someone put some snout ash in your rosie? Makes you put on that wry face, doesn't it? Well, that's what the slag does. Everything they've ever read in a linen or a clever-clever book held upside down they've got—all wrong. Go into the Cavalryman—it's the slag's Boodle's. Ever seen the super card-grafter got up from head to toe in Woolworth's? Well, he's there, ordering half a bitter in the corner, trying not to look at himself in that scrubby old mirror with 'Draught Guinness' written on it. Mothy old waistcoat (with a sort of *fob* thing, dear God!) a *string tie*, chef's sponge-bags with three creases in the front (probably slept on them in Waterloo Station and had a nightmare). But hear him talk—and Jesus! he's got four long ones in the bank and a baccarat game all set up for tonight (come to a rub, though, you'll find it's somewhere along the Baize), the lot. Then there're all those terrible old birds in black slickers got up like the wild ones or the bad seed or something, crackling and popping like damp firelighters, dim, boozy old bosoms all jumbling and flooping about like elephants at feeding time—or else the trim sort, gone all *prim* and *coy* because they've *made it* (do you *mind*!) living with

21

the superthinker leaning against the pillar over there, some grubby Rachmaninoff scrubbing his ginger beard with a claw like a Victorian paperweight. The terrible thing about the slag, though, is that they actually *survive*, down to the Yanks and French being such pushovers and thinking this must be London's *left bank*, when it's nothing but a grafter's paradise. . . . Oo, I get so livid listening to the slag trying to pass itself off as grafters: they couldn't graft their way out of a wet paper bag—they've never done an honest day's graft in their lives. They'd turn up at the Ritz to see a punter with last week's socks on, they're that daft. I tell you, it's the *slag* that's made Chelsea a dirty word. Left to the morries, it really would *be* something. Mind, I'd have nothing against the slag if it'd just stick to its silly old daubing or drooling out Rimbaud at a snap party. But oh dear no. Graft's the new gravy train so the silly things have climbed aboard—last—and then when they've broken all the springs and brought it all to a grinding halt they stare around like moody old brontosauruses and want to know where the *graft* is! Anyone'd think it was the Klondike gold rush all over again; you can't just kindly tell them to keep off the grass, that this thing needs *brains* . . . oo, I get so effing *cross* I could go moodying on for hours about them!

But for the morries, as I was saying, it's gold kettles, the jam-jar and a kosher pad: keep going till the next touch, no matter what, and a good solid heavy like Chas to deal with the writ-servers. . . . The point about the morries is, they've got brains and initiative . . . none of this moodying about in bed all day like the layabouts, dreaming about the withering away of the state or something. Morries are sharp to bed at 6 a.m. and up at noon, no larking about. The thing is, we've had this expensive education; Marchmare even made Oxford for a couple of terms, and the Archbubble got a kosher law degree. So you see what we can do.

And we've got contacts, though we take a rather odd attitude to them, maybe. Marchmare summed it up best when he said to me one day: 'You know, morrie, there's never any point in remembering who anyone is unless it's down to biz and they're rich enough to be really worth hating . . . it's extraordinary how they come drifting downstream and fall straight on to *that* hook.'

I never knew anyone who could hate quite like Marchmare. I remember we were doing some biz near Munich last summer and we were on our way to the Czech frontier for something we hadn't got and had to have. One morning we got a flat tyre (we were using my Jag) so we took it to the garage and told the krauts to get at it; then we nipped smartly off for a bevvy. Once we'd got well bevvied up Marchmare let go. Leaning forward he told me: 'How I hate everyone, morrie.' Very thin, is Marchmare, and very elegant and young and kosher-looking—a gemini same as me, with a boat-race that can slip straight from looking like an angel's to a snake's. I believe he really could palm a dodgy kite on the Assistant Commissioner or stick a fork (but he did this once) into the hand of a moody punter at a chemmy game while the latter was scooping up the chips saying well, well, fancy, eight beats nine. Marchmare's had more publicity in the linens down to general larking and going ahead than you could shake a stick at, and his real speciality is the old international moody. When he's in London he leaps in and out of the bath at Rome Street, S.W.3, our gaff (but he's never dirty, Marchmare isn't, not even when he's been all night with a bird —very sinister, somehow), and then he likes to put on a bit of flash, so he goes swimming up and down the King's Road in his Chevvy convertible with the electric hood, throwing fireballs at the slag, parking this dreadful great orange-and-cream jamjar ('thoroughly nasty and vulgar, dear', as my grandmother would have said) slap under a no-parking sign . . . more front than Buckingham Palace. He hates the law, and, believe me, it's mutual. Never done bird, our Marchmare, but sus clings to him like an aura. There was one time the law thought it'd got him down to kiting, and it went all the way up to the High Court, but the judge was his mother's cousin and a lot of strings were pulled nearly out of their sockets, so it was no go for Old Bill.

Besides, he was only nineteen. But, see what I mean, the difference between the slag and the morries? Anyway, back to this day in krautland: I'm a bit older than Marchmare so I lecture him a bit, because I think he sometimes pushes the boat out a bit far when he's off on this hating kick and saying things like the above.

'Oh, shup,' he says to my lecturing, 'moody old you.'

'Shup shelf.'

'Oo, how I do hate everyone!'

'But why, morrie?'

He doesn't know, though, except obscurely it's all down to Mum, who certainly does, from what I can hear, seem to have dragged him up a bit strange. 'Listen,' he says, 'how much is your father worth?'

'I don't know,' I say, moodying; 'about eighty grand.'

'Habits?'

'What do you mean, habits?'

'You know what I mean,' he says, all impatient; 'where's his office, what time does he reach it, what time does he leave. See what I mean? Slip it into him in the street.'

'No, morrie.'

'Yellow streak down your back, morrie.'

'Maybe.'

'I would.'

'Why don't you, then?'

'Not enough reddy in it in my case.' He sighs. He isn't joking. A real morrie conversation in the heart of the Tirol.

Moments like these, though, when we're relaxing in the sun, life feels good. We're a team. Down to biz there'd never be any grassing. We'd never grass on each other even at the end of time, nor even long after time had run out, as it threatens to sometimes: we're not like the slag, who start grassing even before they've been whacked, soon as they get their collar felt—not even after a right punch-up from the law in a little granite room, not for a ten-stretch. Would you believe it, I think it's something to do with being *gentlemen*—the last relics of romance, which always looks a bit grubby close up like the Spanish Civil War or something—out with the flashing rapiers and all that Errol Flynn stuff. Anyway, it's kicks: Drake with his genes turned upside down, inside out; a new *sort* of Drake with pressure on him from all over the manor—pressure from the law, the income-tax boys, from the middle classes who hate us and the working classes, not to mention the oafos, the things who hate us . . . they all want to squeeze out the upper classes, strip us, put us out of our agony. We're supposed to be in an impossible situation nowadays, too useless to exist: products of our parents who live on the shreds of their inheritances like Marchmare's and mine do, and keep up a pointless front. But just because we've absorbed all that doesn't mean to say us morries are the same. Maybe we're a bit rotten (maybe: do you *mind*!) but we've still got our energy, brains, education—we're all dressed up and nowhere to go, and they've taxed us out of our loot, but we've got expensive tastes and we need the loot so out we go and get it. Mind, that's not to say I've got much sympathy for most of the ice-creams I was at school with, who keep on pretending that something that doesn't exist any more still does. Would you believe it? I've known squares I was at school with (prefects, monitors, scholarship-winners, all that crap) take jobs in INDUSTRY, as *management trainees*! Oh, morrie, do me a favour, will you? You know what that is? It's a formal death sentence. I don't say one or two of them don't make it, but *oo*! the *convulsions*! No, no, Marchmare, the Archbubble and I—we know we can't win, but we're going to make sure we don't lose. The game we play, it's got its risks, but it's a heady, intoxicating game; better than nine-to-fiving it and sex, cocktails and rows in a pseudo-tudo cottage near Sevenoaks. At least we're *living*. So life's a jungle. So it's a terrible thing.

We're knockers, that's what we are. We swim into a shop in Bond Street. Need a tie? Have a dozen. Knock, morrie. More front than Buckingham Palace! Form dodgy companies. Knock. Knock at nightclubs, restaurants, swimming-pools, the South of France, chemmy in Paris . . . knock knock knock—hundreds of hammers whizzing through the air, hard bronze knocking hammers to sling through society's glassy front . . . try it sometime. But it's not really as easy as it looks, and then there's the angst: if we've got one bankruptcy petition floating about looking for a home we've got ten. The first time it frightens you, and you go bleating for help and everyone screams with laughter. Then you catch on and find a punter to get you out of trouble. Then you knock him. Or you go to the wall. So I've marked your card, morrie: I've told you just who we are and what the slag is and what morries are—so you know what the score is from here on in, as the Americans say. All we've got is brains— and I don't mean the kind that spill out of your ear-hole when you soar out on top of it all for a moment in front of a juke-box along the Baize or in a bar behind the Via Nazionale with a drop of Stock 84. As for Old Bill, the law, who can't leave us alone for a minute, true he's a groove behind. But only *one* groove. Sometimes, all unexpected, he's a groove in front. Old Bill's no fool, as many a morrie now sweeping on the twos up at the Scrubs'll tell you with tears in his eyes. Right, then. Here's the scene: we've seen the new boat of the proletariat, all gleaming eyes and scribbling away nineteen to the twelve over the river in Battersea Park, *and* everyone's had more than a good clock at the new middle class: birds all white eyes and duffel with ten quid nicked out of Ma's housekeeping on the mantelpiece (so they're an heiress) and a hot crotch in their jeans eloping with edwards. O.K.—now let's get the twirl out and swing back the old baronial doors and have a look at Britain's great new *upper* class—broke, and with a fly in the ointment: Marchmare, the Archbubble and me.

. . . I remember scraps of moody dialogue: 'Ain't he square!' 'Get *you*, dearie!' 'Ooever seen such camping about and going ahead?' It was outside the jeelied-eel stall round the back of the Double 5 Club over at Brixton. Then Marchmare cut someone up with his latchkey, the Archbubble had his Greek glasses bust and then we were into my jam and going like the hammers, fireballs drifting out the whole way made by lighting bits of linen-draper all bloody. I remember we went to Winston's, the greatest nightclub on earth (also the hottest) in Clifford Street, and Marchmare walloping a strange bird he later charvered. And sometime that night I must have met someone and said something, because the next morning, while we were still spark out with the worst hangover on earth, quite early there was a phone call for me and we were off.

2

I T WAS like this. We'd all been complaining for weeks how poor biz was and the tightness of money. The Archbubble had been going ahead like mad, sparring with the resident heavy and vowing not to show himself again till something was done about it. Marchmare and I felt the full weight of his Attic wrath. But what could we do? You can't *make* biz happen, but that didn't help: even the hoods over at the Tealeaf were giggling at us, and it was no good poncing about in there with our Savile Row knickers and knocking down gin-and-tonic when there were no wages—hardly marching money, even. I was two payments behind with my jam, and Marchmare had lent his to some slag for a ton who had smashed it up abroad on some pitiful slag grafting expedition. A rich boiler or two, bent poker games with Marchmare and me lamping each other's broads . . . everyone knocked anyway and the heavy had to go and beat wages out of them. We had a good bit owing down to the old, but they were just slag punters and couldn't pay even when we put the frighteners in. The Archbubble had had a lot of trouble down to a raid on his chemmy game a while back, so even that was out, and the poor old firm was going dead unsteady.

I ought to explain at this point that at the time I wasn't living full time at our gaff. I couldn't afford to, so I'd moved in for a night or two with an old boiler I had on my hands who fancied herself a bit at the painting lark. She even sold a few—but the real wages came from her old dad who paid up regularly from the grave, which suited the pair of us. She'd been married to a dodgy Italian diplomat, though she was British herself; but he'd been caught scarpering with the Embassy's petty cash and was now busy doing a six in the Aracoeli in Rome . . . isn't it simply extraordinary how every single person one knows seems to be mixed up in some kind of deviation or other somewhere? Anyway, this aged scrubber, Mrs. Marengo (I always called her 'Mrs.' even when I was charvering her, she was so old, forty) was a game old bird. I never leaked anything to her, of course, and when I used to pull out a couple of ton in beehives, which I often inadvertently did, I'd tell her it was down to rent-collecting in Balls Pond Road. I actually had a dodgy property company called As-You-Like-It Investments Ltd., which I'd taken over from Marchmare, and being a director of it served as a handy front when one was working the income-tax fiddle and that kind of lark—though wages there would never have produced the two ton referred to, unless you divided it by ten first —and I'd got a stack of complaints, rates demands, dilapidations (that was funny: the whole lot was falling down!) a mile high, which were sent to the office address in St. James's where I never went any more, for the simple reason I no longer had a lease there, down to not paying the duke. Anyhow, darling old Mrs. Marengo was one of those fairly rare birds—a dead old grafter herself, only she wouldn't admit it, like one of those old dames with dentures—and if for any reason I had to have a hideaway down to the trickle of writs becoming a sudden flood, she was always good for it, and once, when she had a sheet in the wind, she even let me hide in a cupboard down in the bedroom at the studio while she flogged her old Hungarian count—a great lark, and something I'd never actually seen before. Sometimes I don't know where I'd have been for general laughs and going ahead if it hadn't been for Mrs. Marengo. The morries always laugh at me because I enjoy charvering boilers, but, as I told them and tell you, I don't see anything wrong with it. Of course, they look terrible, but I'd much rather have a go at them, who really enjoy it, than one of those dumb birds, got up like the

29

dog's dinner and talking more cobblers to the square inch than the bishop on confirmation day. You just ought to hear some of them—going off about Sartre, method acting, Ionesco, Colin Wilson or the Redbrick Writers, whatever their particular kick happens to be . . . all stuff I read ages ago and, with respect, know considerably more about, down to my wearing my head in its proper place and not between my scotches like a sporran. I used to have lots of rows with Marchmare on the subject of bird. He went for the type I've just described for the simple reason that they went potty about *him*. This was because he treated them the way they wanted to be treated—that is, badly—cutting them right down to size from the word go and making them look dead small when it came to the snob angle; the simple reason being he knew everyone from the Duchess of Riofrio upwards and downwards, had made a bomb out of most of them and charvered them into the bargain.

Anyway, these slag birds used to go trotting upstairs with him at night over at the morries' gaff, arses wagging and bristols going, all complete with black slickers and stockings, no make-up, the lot, with that dreadful cream-puff dumb look on their boats, and come staggering down the next morning in a bath-towel, looking like a cross between a piece of Salvador Dali tomfoolery and a torpedoed battleship. I'd descend with my boiler, the Archbubble with his spade, and by eleven o'clock we'd be all ready for breakfast: tomato ketchup on a bit of ready-sliced bread and tepid tea made by the heavy. Then Marchmare would hide his bird's knickers in the loo or somewhere, or hang them out of the window where the neighbours in the council flats could see them; then the writ-servers would start knocking and the heavy would have his hands full for a bit (some of those Yiddish boys never know when they've had enough) and by midday if they hadn't cleared off we'd be out of the gaff over the back wall, pick up the jamjar from the lock-up garage we hired two blocks away, then off to the Ritz in our dayglo school ties for a drink among the fouls, and the morries were all ready for the day's graft.

Back to Mrs. Marengo—all I wanted to say about her for the time being was that while the firm was going through this dodgy period I've been telling you about I thought I'd pop down to her studio one evening with a view to putting the bite on for some reddy.

But Mrs. Marengo was in no mood to part.

'I'm sick to death of it,' she said.

'I know, darling.'

'Do you like my latest painting?' she said, going over to the easel, which she'd covered over with a duster. This wasn't what I'd come for; still, they have to be humoured. She disclosed something that looked like the exploded diagram of a clock-work gramophone, bits of stuff that looked like machinery, or possibly sick, whirling outwards from a sinister off-centre crimson blob, the whole splodged on to a grey ground. Don't ask me what it was, dearie; it certainly wasn't art. I was on the point of bursting out with what I really thought of it when I suddenly remembered what I'd come for. So I said, learily:

'You still need a few more lessons, I think, dolling.'

'But you like it,' she said, in that definite voice.

'Not like, no, darling,' I said. 'Frightened.'

The old devil was pleased. '*Good*,' she said, giving me a drink. 'It's very Freudian, of course,' she continued, when we were comfortably settled somehow or other on each other's knees.

'Of course it is,' I said, eyeing the dreadful thing. 'What's that crimson bit in the middle mean?'

'Mean?' she said. 'I don't know what it means,' and added after about five minutes off for moody thought: 'It doesn't mean *anything* in a *linear* sense.'

'No, I *know*,' I said. 'It's a *circular, dimensional* concept.'

Do you know? The old darling simply threw her arms round me and *cried* for joy. 'You've said it for me, you sweetheart you,' she choked, 'the canvas has spoken'—yes, she even shed a tear or two, when all I'd done was to repeat the things I'd picked up from her over hundreds of previous loot-tapping visits. Really, boilers are simply potty. And I'd like to get my motives for having her on perfectly straight: the sweet old dear couldn't paint for potatoes, so what was the good of trying to tell her what one thought about *painting*, of all things? All it did was keep her out of mischief, and the old Hungarian whatnot sucked it down too, because all *he* wanted was for her to beat him, which she did heartily, though with a mystified look. 'Because, of course,' she said to me one day rather shyly, 'actual *sex* with him would be simply impossible, wouldn't it? I mean, he's so strange.'

'What you ought to do,' I said, as best I could for giggling, 'is put the bite on the old ice-cream.'

'Oh, I couldn't,' she says, blushing. 'Anyway, he hasn't any money.'

'That's all you know,' I rejoined hotly; 'he's sitting on a bomb.'

But she simply didn't know how to set about it. Poor Mrs. Marengo: she was already settling down into middle age like a wrecked dredger I once saw on the mudflats at Tilbury—with her circle of pasty old devotees, the *Observer* after lunch on Sundays in this kosher studio, walks in the park and patting young Portuguese poets on the head . . . all she could do to keep young was charver me and get helplessly drunk every now and then after she'd had a letter from her ex-Long-Range-Desert-Group lover who lived in Eire and was oh most dreadfully square and had a plastic hip down to a parachute accident. 'I really love him,' she'd moan (*when* she'd had it from me, not before).

'Well, why don't you marry the old geezer, then?' I'd say.

But it seemed it wasn't as easy as that; he was married already with three kids, and anyway was a Catholic. . . . I don't know: it's hard to work up much sympathy for people who tangle with the religion kick *and* marry—I mean, they've only themselves to thank if they get in a muddle, haven't they? And don't talk to me about the Catholics after the Spanish bird I got mixed up with on that tape-recorder lark. Still, whenever this geezer made that hazardous trip across the Irish Channel I'd always try to be there for a bit; he was quite loyal, really, and it wasn't that I wanted to spoil his fun, just give him a bit of a shock and show him he'd got competition. Anyway, when I'd arrive he used to clock me and look all dim and moody and leave go her hand which he'd been holding on the sofa, looking all over like a mothy aged old secretary-bird I once saw at the zoo. Down to his plastic insert and that he didn't perform too well . . . all in all it was a diminuendo version of the sun also rises. However, he'd soon cheer up when he saw I didn't mean any harm; we'd have a few drinks at her place and then he'd take the pair of us out to dinner. Thereupon I'd get a bit pissed and let off a lot of stuff by Yeats and Eliot, then he'd get dead pissed—and at about the same time get the needle to poor old Mrs. Marengo, who would start going all droopy and wringing her hands. Then he'd pay up like the Oirish gentleman he was, we'd take a taxi back to her gaff and I'd have a heart and pop off to Winston's. And he'd *always* have smacked her one when I came back to see her next day. Oo! a terrible fourpenny he'd have given her, a real parachutist's smack right on the kisser; a great blue-and-black jaw she'd have, halfway out over the Thames, poor old darling. And you know why? All because, I discovered, that just as he'd *at last* worked himself up for a bit of an effort, she'd pass out straight under his nose, and out of sheer disappointment he'd pick her up and whack! and then there'd be top screaming and shouting and going ahead.

Well, one way and another, there's Chelsea for you. It won't win a prize . . . *la vie artistique* . . . I think it's a crying shame, myself. Because it's nothing but slag, come to a rub, moody old nymphos like Mrs. Marengo, morries and aged queans beating each other black and blue and the ponces all killing themselves laughing outside the door and picking up the reddy as the aged come out looking a bit ashamed now they've had their moment of mythomania, and a bit nervous of the ponces who'd shive them without thinking if the aged ones tried to knock for their presents for the girls (or boys). That's all Chelsea is; but try telling it to the butcher's, baker's and stockbroker-maker's sons and daughters all over the land who come belting up to London on the Penzance Flier or the Glasgow Snapdragon the second they're out of the nursery, and they'll go all *moody* and *Beardsley drawing* and look down their sniffers at you and say: 'Aeouw! but *yeouw* don't understand!' and camp about all over the place. Poor bastards—just more slag . . . and then the next thing you know you pick up the linen and there they are in court and not even on page one, down to having it away with someone's spoons, and then it's all moans and groans and two years' probation and back to Mum and going off about being caught up in the *Chelsea vortex*, poor tortured *souls*.

Anyway, down at Mrs. Marengo's this night it wasn't a bit of good her saying she was sick of handing out the loot. As I pointed out, I wasn't a layabout, I was a morrie, and many was the time over our long association when I'd had a touch and been handy to have around when it came to paying the duke with my beehives down to a bit of archbishop. Tonight, though, she was being very difficult to play, and she was dead randy besides, which was a bore—because I was meeting the morries later on; they'd marked my card there was a new dance-hall been opened over at Peckham and we were dying to have a butchers and lamp all the new bird. No, it meant charvering Mrs. Marengo for a kick-off, and then seeing what was to be had out of it. I looked her over. She wasn't looking a bit tasty, but then, if you're a boiler man, that's just part of the package, isn't it? as they say in the States. At least the old bristols were still more or less okay, but the rot had set in something horrible with her hampsteads and scotches, not to mention the boat. Still, there was nothing for it, so I filled up with red wine, to throw up a kind of Maginot Line of euphoria to cower behind.

But, Jesus! It was like drinking a Molotov cocktail!

'What's *this*?' I wailed, setting up a right scream.

'Algerian red, darling,' cooed the old devil, her homespun skirt up all over her knees.

'I can see that,' I shouted, 'the six-and-nine touch! It's not fit to drink,' I moaned, and scrambled out from under her and soared away to the off-licence and nearly didn't come back, but I was broke, so I finally bought a quart of grappa that would have made grandma flutter in her bloomers. After about an hour, though, Mrs. Marengo had noshed her half down without a qualm and I realized my hour had come. Still, hopping into bed while she did obscure things to herself in the bathroom I saw something poking out from under the radio beside me and on principle had it away rather sharply. Naturally, it was her bank statement dated that morning, and there was a bomb in it. Birds really are so clumsy with papers. Charvering her my mind was of course revolving schemes for knocking her loose from a bit of this for marching money while I mooed and groaned and made all the noises that long experience indicated were the right ones. But suddenly, at the peak of Mrs. Marengo's moment (as she called it), I couldn't contain myself any more.

'This two hundred and nine quid eight shillings I see you've got,' I said briskly, 'what about it?'

'Finish me, finish me,' Mrs. Marengo was groaning, in a voice that would have been a credit to Garbo and dated back to the same. Then she said 'What?' in a very different voice, all about trout, and would have sat up if I hadn't been squashing the old bird.

There was a right bit of angst, I can tell you, but in the end she peeled off a score. 'And you said you were broke, dear!' I chided her.

'I couldn't possibly make love to you now,' said Mrs. Marengo frigidly, having just made it.

'Good,' I said, delighted, and starting pulling on my shoes. Then the blower went. Quick as a flash I copped for it and pruned down the mouthpiece: 'Good evening, Chelsea C.I.D.'

A strangled voice the other end said: 'Er—oh. I wanted a Mrs. Marengo.'

'Wrong number, mate,' I said, and then added: 'What was the name again?'

'A Mrs. Marengo. Olive.'

'No olives here, I'm afraid,' I said, fighting off Mrs. Marengo with one finger. I waited a minute till the geezer the other end was just going to ring off then said: 'Oh, wait a minute—this is

Mrs. Marengo's house. Yes. We're investigating a few irregularities. Charge is keeping a bawdy house.'

'Olive! My God!!' roared the voice at the other end, and would you believe it? I suddenly realized it was the eternal love speaking from faraway old Eire. Having thus created a nice little bit of angst, I then handed over to Mrs. Marengo, who had top fun sorting it all out while I got dressed. I was halfway downstairs, in fact, when she halted me by the simple method of seizing me by the hair. Goodness, she was cross!

'I'll have back that twenty pounds,' she said in her fruitiest voice.

'Oh, don't be a potty old bird,' I said, wrenching myself free and kissing her on the topknot, and was gone. Into the jamjar, over to the gaff in time for this meet with the morries after all, and then down to the dance-hall, which ended up with the angst I described before, with a trip to the Beehive and then a punch-up at the jellied-eel stall with these dinges saying we were square and then away to Winston's. I got so high that I talked to someone without even remembering who it was, with the result I get this phone call at the gaff at Rome Street, where I'd passed out.

3

A LOT of ice-creams seem to think real life villainy is just like the movies, where the whole thing's timed to run ninety minutes and everyone gets let off in the end anyway because the dear old super's a family man himself and the judge was the illegitimate son of a grand duke. They think one deviator just somehow meets another and then wham! someone has at you with a wooden shooter and then cut to the visiting-room at the Scrubs.

That's all *they* know.

This geezer on the blower was so roundabout that he sounded deadly sus; in fact, if the law had been on the wire that morning tapping us (and who knows they weren't?) they'd have had a right old giggle when they played it all back, and would doubtless have tipped off darling old Det. Sgt. Plinth who always drops over to see us whenever there's a bit of angst about anything. I've heard the slag say Plinth's bent—just the stupid sort of half-baked thing you'd expect the slag to say. We've never found him anything of the kind. He carries the whole burden of the honour of the force on his shoulders, and it shows in his temper, too, which is murderous if he thinks we're trying to blag him.

Anyway, this ice-cream talks in a low throaty voice which is so obviously disguised, morrie, I could laugh, and keeps calling me Mr. Potter. Well, it's an original name, anyway.

'Got something for you, maybe,' he says.

'What sort of thing, maybe?' I says, trying to fight the drink out of my eyes.

'*You* know, the second-hand jams, like we was on about last night.'

Now if there's one thing I'm quite certain of, that thing is that I've never discussed second-hand jams with anyone in my life, except up along Warren Street on one of my courtesy visits to Dodge O'Toole on the way back from my rent-collecting— never, let alone in Winston's when I'm loaded. Clock about in my mind as I will, though, I can't remember what the hell I *was* on about; so a nasty inner voice like Andrews Liver Salts keeps telling me it may be the law. Still, it seems he's dead keen on a meet, so, biz being slack, I think oh nothing to it and suggest the Admiral up west at half past seven, whereupon he says O.K. and signs off, having told me to be on the look-out for a geezer with a white buttonhole. Do you mind! However, as I'm putting the phone down a most peculiar feeling, which I've got to know quite well, shoots through me; it tells me six things at once, which must be why it's called the sixth sense. It says watch it, paydirt, villainy, law, foreign parts and 44X angst, whereupon I turn a bit cold and fuzzy inside on *top* of the hangover—but also dead merry in an indescribable way, so that I decide on a bath and a nice clean shirt with narrow cuffs. But I sit on in the chair for a minute staring out, and it's a kosher-looking day outside the gaff too. Early June, and the trees that struggle up out of the forecourt (and the 'To Let' sign, because we're just squatting here) in front of Rome Street are swimming with green and wasps and birds. I get up and look out of the window and there is my loyal jam squatting in front of the house all fat and comforting with its teaspoonful of gas in the tank. I'm on the point of going all moody about money or rather the lack of it, which is why you must never never think, when the door flies open and in tumbles March-mare characteristically got up in his leopard-skin slippers.

'Morrie!' he shrieks. 'Loot!'

'Brilliant!' says I. 'What's it down to?'

He gives off a withering look. 'Dodgy poker of course, what else? Sometimes I think you're square.'

'In reddy?'

'Too right!' he screams and lobs half a ton in beehives through the air and we scramble for it and I get most of it, but finally we split it down the middle smartly before the Archbubble has a chance to get down and claim his whack on top for knowing about it. I'm about to stuff my pony in my kick when he adds: 'That's eighty you owe me, with that fifty-five down to the old, morrie.'

Suddenly I feel my luck dead in, like fancying a bird, running through me all hot and I have a desire to bet up which must never be said no to.

So I say: 'Play you for this pony I got, morrie.'

'You're on,' says he, all brightened up in that second as though he'd that moment got up from a feather bed after eight hours' solid kip instead of having been all that night bending the broads for the benefit of some half-wide mug. So we whip a table into the middle of the drum and I get out a *new* pack of cards from the sideboard (the sort you can't unstick the wrapping of, put all the aces back to back and then stick up again).

'What'll we play?' says I, settling down and lighting a snout and trying not to feel like old scythe-and-bones.

'One pack dealer's choice,' he says, minces all gleaming.

I start to shuffle while Marchmare tears up old linens for chips, the Archbubble having lent his for a chemmy game a night or so previous.

'How much the bits?'

'Bob each, morrie.'

He tears up fifty quids' worth.

'Cut for deal.'

Marchmare cuts high.

'What'll we play, morrie?'

'Baseball of course. Too early for five-card stud.'

Everyone knows baseball. Two downwards, one up, three and

nine are wild, red three doubles the pot, four gets a free card, and last card down.

'Bob ante,' says Marchmare. Then: 'Bet a quid blind,' when he deals and sees he's turned an ace upwards. Mine's only an eight. Still, I look nervously in the hole and goodness there's an ace and a black three there—a toployal pair of aces. So I follow his pound and raise him half a bar; he flips me a four and then another four and then a *nine*, so I'm full house aces before I can say Shakespeare in three languages and he deals himself a king. Two pairs to bet, so I bet two quid and he raises me five and I raise him ten because that's the kind of ice-cream I am and also because I've gone potty-feeling, but cool too, and I can feel it, luck, running through me like the second Hine at La Preserve. Then he deals himself a queen and then suddenly I see my God! they're all *diamonds*, ace, king, queen and God knows *what* in the hole, and in spite of my feeling lucky it suddenly begins to look a bit dodgy and I look very close to see if he's bending them. Suppose he makes royal straight flush? Anyway, he follows my bet of ten cool as Kerouac and deals me crap and himself the three of hearts. He doubles the pot and there's thirty-five nicker on the baize in reddy. Then, Jesus, he deals me the other three.

'I'll have to go light, morrie,' says I, doubling and marking it on the card—and that makes seventy quid and yours truly to bet, so I think oh hell and bet fifteen because it's too late to pull out now anyhow; but I think maybe my luck's not too kosher after all: his hand must be fabulous because I've got four eights showing and a pair of aces in the hole or five eights, whichever you like. Still, none of my dodgy thoughts show on my boat, at least I hope not. He deals himself another *nine*, which makes him royal straight flush bar one card and *two* cards still to go.

'Bet you ten,' he says.

'Up you twenty.'

'Up you forty.'

I've got writer's cramp with the card.

'Deal.'

I get a six and my heart drops plonk through my suède casuals; but Marchmare gets deuce, no use. Still me to bet with my fours. What can I do? I up him another fifteen, don't I, and there's a hundred and ten quid in the pot. But he ups me twenty again. Last card comes face down and I just manage to look casually at mine and see it's ace of clubs. Now for it—three wild cards and a pair of aces makes five aces, a perfectly *fabulous* hand, the sort of hand you see maybe one game in thirty. I watch Marchmare's eyes, their funny dull agate colour, flit over his cards and something tells me *I've won—he hasn't made royal straight* and I leap in with half a ton, but he stacks, looking very choked. When he sees my five aces he nearly goes potty. I haul in the loot, subtract the fifty-five I was into him for from what's on the card and he pays me half the rest. So, from being dead skint at getting-up time, I've now got ninety-five quid in the bin.

And that's not all this fabulous morning! Just as I'm getting out the vera for a celebration bevvy, in comes Chas the frightener and says, looking at us wall-eyed, sort of one eye on each of us:

'Geezers to see you two.'

'Well, now *that's* something new, isn't it?' says Marchmare sarcastically, as he's still choked.

Light dawns on Chas. 'Oh, it's all right,' he says depressedly, lifting one leg and scratching his bottle, 'it's down to his motor,' and nods at Marchmare.

Now that's this orange-and-cream Chevvy I was on about before, and there are one or two very dodgy things about this motor which you ought to know. The whole transaction, as the Official Receiver would say, began with an ice-cream we done a bit of biz with coming to see us one morning. He lives out Harpenden way and looks rather square, but actually he nearly topped a screw up at the ville with a mailbag needle when he was doing a three there for g.b.h. But now he's—well, not six-and-eight exactly, but settled down very cosy with a hand in a dance-hall which brings in steady wages, though he's still not above a bit of screwing here and there; also he does a bit with the jamjar lads on Warren Street. Anyway, he arrives in this huge great jam and says simply do we want it, half a ton down and nothing to pay. Well, we get him a bit bevvied and finally we prize him loose from the priceless info that the knocking company the jam's down to is shortly going to fold—so all we've got to do is take over the motor on a new agreement, without of course (and this is where the blag comes in) letting the h.p. geezer notice that he hasn't voided the original agreement with the hood we're taking it over from. Well, with a front like ours (director of twelve companies, etc., etc.) this sort of thing is child's play. Is the jam hot? we ask sceptically. 'Course it's not hot. Then what's the snag? There must *be* a snag, we argue sensibly. Well, it turns out the snag is that he's expecting a john any day now down to a bit of rural screwing where the fencing came unstuck, the owner of his dance-hall got himself bottled and razored in a punch-up over at the Elephant—proper carve-up and won't be out of the hospital for weeks, meanwhile no wages and he needs the half-ton for marching.

Come to a rub we take the wretched thing . . . and of *course*, darling, it's absolutely Marchmare one hundred per cent, in and out and through and through; and for *months* he fills it up with bird and glides up and down the King's Road in this *thing*, my dear, that looks like Anne Boleyn's ghost with a hatful of search-lights in her teeth, and he wraps it round half the telephone poles in G.B. and there's deadly aggravation from the law down to its being untaxed, uninsured and the brakes don't work and the power steering's bust down to all those great strong hoods that've had it; but it's tremendously *flash*, with more front than Buckingham Palace . . . only smoke pours out of its fanny at the back and only the other day he had another flat and we had to get one of our punters with a garage to come and pick it up and dust it over and put it back on its wheels . . . a real morriemobile. In the death, though, it went the way of all the best bent jams, because, as I was saying, Marchmare lent it to this hatful of slag for a ton down and it streamed off for the Channel and points south, pistons knocking, tyres slapping, streams of writs, law, parking tickets, traffic wardens, affidavits and Uncle Tom Cobley and all after it. First we heard it caught fire in Parigi, next it hit a rondpoint in Torremolinos doing ninety plus: it would keep breaking *down*, but it was early summer and slag-time for going abroad, and the entire contents of the Hautboy were tumbling over themselves to be first to cop on to this jam, and we let the slag have it for a ton and wasn't it a super laugh on our deadliest enemy the slag?

And now the slag have brought the motor back, poor old darling, properly clapped out, and want their *ton* back! There, if I went on all night I couldn't give you a better example of how *stupid* the slag is. But if you've ever seen an ice-cream all got up in Woolworth's gear propped up in the buffet at Paddington waiting for a millionaire to come along and say 'How much d'you want, son?' which is the slag's idea of graft, you'll see what I mean.

In the death, anyhow, we all go down with the heavy and nick the jam away from the slag after a mild punch-up which is mostly just the scrubbers in the back wailing and waving their gunny-sacks and screaming and going ahead. The documents were all in Marchmare's name, anyway, so exit the slag, come to a rub, murmuring against us, as the Old Testament rather patly puts it.

4

THE Admiral, as everybody knows, is a dreadful little gaff, which is why everyone never goes there because it's as square as the dear old Admiral himself (Admiral Teitelbaum of the Whitechapel Navy, I shouldn't wonder). It's off behind upper Regent Street and like a bank-clerk's notion of a winter cruise gone sour in a blob of aspic; and the reek of stale middle-aged slag, wet macintoshes and beer contrast oddly with the burnt-pokerwork observations stuck about which tell you that the loo is on the midshipmen's deck—in a nutshell, it's the one place where the law wouldn't stick out like a sore thumb, which makes it O.K. for biz, as the law seems to think that biz is never done anywhere except in the Hautboy or the Tealeaf, and those two gaffs have more ears stuck around the walls than a Cocteau film.

Anyway, penetrating this dreary drum and ordering a gin-and-tonic, which arrives without any lemon or ice, I take a swallow of the horrid tepid thing and gaze mildly about. Needless to say, there's no sign of the contact, but after a minute the door opens and in comes the white buttonhole whistling through his teeth and looking about as different from the general clientele sitting fadedly about with their milk stouts as I do:

> 'Oh, his clobber's deadly sharp
> but he'll never get swinging with a harp'

—a tiny tune I this minute invented. He's in a tweed lavender-mixture suit a bit short round the buttocks like you buy 'em over at Peckham, winklepickers—dark and good-looking in a bashed-about kind of way—hardly surprising, as he's got lots of form and his release ticket said his next stretch would be a seven-to-ten corrective training . . . a small compact head, dangerous like a bullet, and a general look of dislike in the minces which tremble a bit in their sockets: all about trout, in fact.

He clocks me and wanders up in a very proper manner, orders a light ale and says very low: 'I'm Mike; bring the vera over here and let's get at it,' and we move over to a small table covered with old beer circles and Admiral Teitelbaum's ship's wheel pontificating on the wall above staring like one of those great eyes in a backdrop for *Ivan the Terrible*, Part Two.

We spend a minute or two in the usual courtesies between deviators—you know, dropping the odd name like Dodge O'Toole or Mr. Cream for flash, and discover we have lots of them in common, and then I think, well, let's cut this, O.K.? and get down to biz. So I says a bit sharply: 'So what's the story?'

His eyes open wide. 'You mean you don't remember?'

Yes—well, I mean it's awkward, isn't it? But I have to admit I was so pooped I couldn't recall a thing.

'A right carve-up,' he mutters, choked. 'You stuck-up poncey lot of bastards,' he adds with a look I don't like. 'I know what it's down to, you've grassed: every time I done bird it's been down to a grass, some effing copper's nark.' He pretends to joke: 'I am G-i-i-no, I ke-e-e-el you.'

'All right,' I says, getting the needle in my turn, 'well, if you thought I was a grass what did you arrange this meet for?'

'Well,' he says, letting go a bit, 'pointofact I had the obbs on you and you come out twenty-two carat and a bit of luck for you.' And he adds: 'Come to a rub, this biz I got in mind needs someone with a bit of brains.'

Now this is a super mark of the loyal in my vocabulary

(besides the pure *flattery* of it, darling) because nearly all petty grafters and deviators claim brains for themselves when mostly they couldn't make head or tail of a kid's copybook. But they don't see themselves that way. *Oh*, no. Left to themselves they'll tell you they're the Einsteins of the underworld and only done bird four times down to some dreadful misunderstanding with the law ('I'm dead sharp, see? But the law's dead agin me, see?') —in fact, just like the slag only less appetizing. Come to a rub, they've no sense of perspective, analysis, limitation—in fact, all they can see in the great mirror of life is a dirty old blob and a few screws, and then they try to make out it's all crystal clear to them and, well, you can tell they're fibbing, can't you?

But Mike isn't a bit like that. 'There's this old international moody to it,' he is saying; and this favourite phrase of March-mare's puts me in mind of him and the Archbubble to put up the exes, the old team, in fact—but, as I'm playing spokesman for them, I've got to be dead careful what I put their names down for, as no one, need I say, wants to get his collar felt and wind up with a judge saying nasty disloyal things which all get in the linens, so that my auntie says 'I always knew it, that boy' and there's top angst at Tumbledown Towers.

'You speak kraut?' says Mike.

'Nishte. Twenty words.'

'Or the other morries?'

I shook my head.

'Frog?' he pursued gamely.

'Well up to frog. And Spanish. Good. Some Eyetie.'

'We'll manage.'

Now I am very curious. 'What's all this down to, then?'

His mouth barely moved: 'Slush.'

Slush! I feel like Colonel Bulbul the day he did two grand on a non-starter at the Tealeaf. Deadly disappointment shoots through. For slush is just hopeless. It's an old old lark and mostly rotten stuff—fact is, most of it wouldn't deceive a kid of six, and so I tell him roundly.

But he shakes his head. 'You haven't seen this.'

'O.K.,' I says, 'let's have a butchers, then.'

'In a minute.'

'It'd better be good slush,' I argue. 'I don't think you quite tumble. There's hundreds of things you've got to check with slush. Paper, serials, what sort of plates they used or was it photos . . . oh, no, no, no.'

'Now listen,' he says. 'They're beehives, this lot, and I tell you they're absolutely twenty-two. None of this photogravure lark. Proper plates.'

'Who the hell made them, then?' says I, still playing the sceptic, as much on principle, though, as anything, as I'm dead broke and am dying for there to be something in it.

But he plays it very cagey. 'It's kraut,' he says off-handedly, but his minces are burning with a deadly gleam El Greco'd've been proud of. 'Dead kosher merchandise. Big deal. Really big.'

'That case,' says I, 'why no contact already?'

'Had one,' he says. A long pause. Finally I can see him take the plunge after all this fancy rapier work and decide to tell me the whole story—in bits, of course. 'Had one,' he says. 'Got grassed, though. Usual thing. Old Bill come and turn his drum right over. But old Bri—well in front. Ships it out to me first, doesn't he?'

'I suppose so,' says I, not fancying old Bri's sport too much.

'Yes,' says Mike reminiscently, 'two days in front he was before he sees old cocked-hat-and-whiskers climbing out of a motor three-handed his place.'

Well, I'm still not committing myself; but there's no harm listening. It's always a bit pathetic hearing about deviators who tripped themselves up.

'Then they whipped him down to the nick on the hurry-up.'

'Which manor?'

'The local nick. Cleg. Right bastard, he is. Law down there, they think he's God in a cardboard hat, they do. "Now, then, Phelps" (that's Bri's last name), says this Cleg. "Make this easy for yourself. Be a big boy. Confess." "Confess

47

what?" says old Bri. "Come on, Phelps lad, now," says this copper, "you know what I mean." "Sorry, Inspector," says our Bri, "don't know what you're on about, I'm sure." "O, now I like your spirit, Phelps," says this copper, all sarcastic, who fancies himself a bit as the old iron duke—he does, I've had to do with him myself—"Yes, I like your spirit, same as I always do when you're nicked and brought down here, but it's no go this time, lad, you been grassed." Now Old Bri's laughing really, see, because no one don't know anything about this slush deal, but he's got his enemies same's we all have, and it turns out some ponce grassed him over bird bekos Bri does a bit in the immoral earnings way on the side (this grass, by the way, we 'ad to go over to the grasses in West Ken—come to a rub, they don't know when he'll be out of hospital: maybe two months, maybe three, maybe not at all, two of Cream's boys put the boot in something 'orrible). Anyway, that's another story. "Well," says this Cleg, "you've had it. Now then, lad, you'll be up for a five-stretch this time, won't you?" "No, I won't," says Bri, with a bit of this spirit Old Bill's been on about, "because I 'aven't done nothink so get well you know what," he adds under his breath —yes, he did, he told me himself. So this inspector waves back some oafo copper—who comes for Bri like a liner in a thick fog off Dogger Bank an' smiles a gentle smile, gentle as a Miles Davis cool number—and says: "No, no, constable, I'm going to give our Brian a fag," an' he leans over and brings out this heavy old snout case, see, as though to offer him one and then *wack!* Oo, an' fetches 'im such a clout! "You what?" says the copper. "I nothing," says Bri—well as 'e can for blood and busted hampsteads—"so clout away." An' so they do, three of um. An' they grill 'im for near on seventeen hours all night an' halfway through next day, but meanwhile it's nishte for the old lumberfeet back at Bri's drum so they as to let 'im go in the death.'

Yes, well there you are, morrie, it's a sobering tale, isn't it? I don't know how many times I haven't heard it, but every time it gives me the butterflies.

'Anyhow,' says I, when I've recovered a bit and had another go at my vera, 'he had this specimen note, did he?'

'The what?'

'Ah, yes, well, you know what I mean: the sample, the merchandise, the slush, the piece of dodgy loot.'

'Oh, that?' says Mike. 'Well, I've got that right here in the kick, me old Chelsea baron,' patting himself on the pocket.

Which puts a different complexion on it.

Meanwhile, though, he is peering around looking worried.

'What is it?' says I.

'Don't like staying same place too long.'

'Nor I.'

'Where to for next one?' says he.

'Well off the manor, if you like. In my motor?'

'If you like,' says he, 'since it's dark.'

So off we go through the June twilight and join the traffic in the Haymarket and presently up through the Park, where the lamps are beginning to twinkle like *Fanny by Gaslight*, Scene One: past the H.P.H. and then out to the Cromwell Road. It's a beautiful cool evening, full of top-loyal-looking bird and full of soulful memories—especially of my childhood when my old man had a kosher residence hereabouts and I was a darling little youth in button-knickers running away from Nanny and being picked up by a copper with a face like an ad for 'Join the Metropolitan Police—A Fine Career', who took me by my little hand and escorted me back to Nanny and wasn't it lovely? She got fired for losing me, which was my whole scheme, maybe. I let Mike drive to see how he handles the jam, and I needn't have worried, he makes a super job of it, whipping it through gaps that a flea with goitre couldn't have made, with an I've-done-all-this-before attitude, which he certainly has, because he starts telling me about his days as a teenager driving for a screwing team. Well, I tune in the radio and get 'Pick of the Pops' and I sing like a maniac because I'm happy about the way this deal is shaping and Mike groans in unison and people who tell you that deviators think of nothing but knocking each other off and loot and so on shouldn't: I'm young and just having a good time and even deviators are human beings, you know—all that stuff about 'I Saw A Human Monster In My Bedroom, says Teenager' you read in the Sunday linens is a lot of tripe—because for the screwsman it's sheer bad luck and means the little mystery's woken up when she wasn't supposed to. And all the while, over the music, we're rabbiting about the most *diabolical* things and I throw a fireball in the shape of a piece of lighted linens under a bus. But miss, and it lands at the feet of some painted old boiler taking her doggie for a walk. Aghast indignation and angst . . . stir her up, though, and off at fifty for the next lights, Mike practising his get-away start which the three-point-four certainly responds to in *no* uncertain way. But at the same time I've already started dissecting and tabulating all the info I've been getting on this slush. Never under-estimate the opponent, secure your base like old Clausewitz said and talk about anything except everything—for if there's one thing certain it is that I'm not going to do any bird down to stupid larking about.

Finally we find a very quiet street and park, switching off all lights. Jams and discussion of slussion go well together, because if you start rabbiting about things like that in a drum there's always a chance of angst, down to that bit about the old ears in the Cocteau film I was on about before.

5

WELL, I don't know if you've ever been passed a dodgy beehive in the half-light of a parked motor—but I can tell you, I've handled enough beehives in my time to know if there's anything wrong with one, just by the feel. Well, this one that Mike passes me; automatically I've taken it, felt it and passed it halfway into my bin before the goddess of reason ups and says: 'Do you mind, that's slush, morrie.'

So I pull out a kosher beehive to compare it with.

'Here,' says Mike, 'take this to it,' and passes me a big screwsman's torch. Then he shouts out: 'Hell it was *good*, daddy-o: it fooled you, just like it'll fool 'em when it goes over the counter at Marks and Sparks!'

I didn't like to say anything square like 'yes' or 'quite' but well, it had. So I switch on the torch and have a good butchers at the two of them lying on my knee. Do you know? You couldn't tell. None of the dye came off it; it wasn't smudged; you could put the two on top of each other and you *still* couldn't tell—there wasn't a detail out of place, not one. There was the correct number of digits in the serial—hell, it was *too* good. I'd never seen slush anything like *this* before: there must've been a great deal of hard work going on for a very long time in a very quiet place far from the madding crowd. In fact, I wasn't quite certain whether the whole thing wasn't a giant con trick—and that Mike was fooling me into thinking the beehive was slush when in fact it was six-and-eight.

'Well,' I said rather breathlessly, like a deb having her first taste of it outside the marquee, 'it's fabulous.'

He gave me an exceedingly cunning glance. 'Haven't spotted it yet, have you?'

It was no good. I had to confess I hadn't.

'Here,' he said, 'gimme that torch.'

With that he spread the two notes out on the seat while I kept a sharp look-out for rubber-soled law.

Looking very carefully where he pointed, and taking quite a long time over it too, I finally spotted where they had bogged the old bloater's signature.

'Yes,' he sighed, 'that's it. But it's beautiful, really beautiful, isn't it?'

It certainly was. It wouldn't have fooled the boys at the Yard or the Bank of England, but it would fool the average bank-clerk; masses and masses of that you could pass before there was so much as a squeak from the righteous, let alone a right scream.

'I'll have to take it away for a bit,' I said at last, still a bit stunned.

'Take it away?' he screams.

'*Si, si,*' I shouted, laughing, '*si, si, Gino, togliere via* to show the other morries. . . . I ke-e-e-el you!'

'Oh, all right,' he grumbles at last, 'stick it in yer bin and up yer chumper. But does it mean we're in biz together?'

Well, of course that's just what it did mean. You know, taking on deviation's just what marriage must be like: come to a rub you've got to trust your instinct; some old bird you hardly know, you decide to get spliced in the middle of a charver some dark old night, and then the next thing you know there's all the relatives with solemn boats standing around and the better or for worse routine.

'Yes,' I said at last, 'but there's still the short history of this slush's life and times that I haven't had yet—and I can't guarantee the other morries till I've seen them. I reckon I know what they'll say, though.'

And do you know? He whoops with glee and gives me a big punch up the kidneys and whips out a pint of Scotch where the torch came from in his smother: 'I am Gi-i-i-i-no! I ke-e-e-e-el you! O.K.,' he continues, when we have had a bit of a gulp, 'one night this Bri I been on about gets next to an Irish. 'E's known this Irish for years and years; noticed he's been slipping backwards and forward to krautland a bit often. Nothing much in that, see? But you know how these things get around on the vine. So one night the Irish and he are back in Bri's gaff after a right old bevvy-up at Aristov's in Greek Street, you know the drum. Bri and he are rabbitin' away about the biz they done together in the past—and it was a right old bit I can tell you, on the Tulse Hill manor mostly, screwin' and that. Then all at once the Irish says: "Want to know what's in these kraut trips I been making?" and Bri says: "Well, I don't mind listenin' if you don't mind tellin' me." "Well," says the Irish, "it's down to slush," and though he don't use these long uppercut words of yours, morrie, he tells Bri it's fa-bu-lous. Which it is, i'n't it? Well, but then the Irish nearly bursts into tears bekos 'e can't 'andle it down to sus. And in the death he says to Bri: "Well, can't you do somethin' about it for me?" Come to a rub, this slush is from the commies and their agent, this kraut called Reisemann, operates from Frankfurt. They've got all their agents lined up to distribute the merchandise when it arrives: now all they need's a little team with a bit of know-how to ship it across in bulk and slip it in here. See? It was the Irish who lined up the distributors before the sus got too hot, an' then Bri tells me all about it an' here I am tellin' you. See? It's big time.'

I could see that from that one beehive. 'How big?' I said.

'First shipment's a quarter of a million.'

'Jesus,' I said.

'Yes, well it's like this. They've got eighty agents set up. Eighties into two hundred and fifty only goes thirty-odd grand, and that's not much to pass over a period in a big city. An' they've got to be quick. This is commie shock tactics. It's not only the slush, you see, it's the—the . . .'

'Demoralizing element,' I supplied.

'Yeeh,' said Mike,' 'I suppose so.'

Yes, well I could see that. I could also see that it was all going to be very difficult and complex. Perhaps dangerous, even. Oh dear.

'Who's going to be paymaster?' I said.

'This Reisemann character.'

'How do we know he won't knock?'

'Well, he'll give you half your cut when he approves you and sets up the deal. In West German marks.'

It sounded rather promising.

'What *is* our cut?'

'A quarter of the total value of the slush—that's to say, a quarter of a quarter of a million.'

I nearly threw a fit, darling! Goodness, it was a frightful lot.

'To split four ways, though,' I said, not batting an eyelid.

'Four?' he said.

'Yes: Archbubble puts up our exes, Marchmare and I do the hard work. You're legman. That makes four, doesn't it? Can you hurt people?' I added, not that I doubted the answer.

'Yeeh.'

'Use a shooter?'

'Oh, do you *mind*,' he said crossly.

'I don't know,' I said, moodying him a bit, 'there's not a lot in it, is there?'

'Not a *lot*?' he screamed. 'Only sixteen grand apiece, that's all!'

'Well,' I said coldly, 'it's not for sitting on my arse, is it?'

But I was on.

6

AFTER Indian nosh at a little gaff in Earls Court we decided to dangle over to Winston's, look for morries, get bevvied up and generally go ahead. This only after a bit of argle-bargle with Mike, though: 'Are you MAD?' he says to me. 'Here we are all set to do biz and then we go belting off to Winston's, weaving about among the tables, taking our little hats off and bowing and saying "Hullo there" and "The loo's the first door downstairs on the right" to all the assembled law?'

'Bruce is no grass; all you find in Winston's apart from the loyals are the respectable having a night out.

Anyway, I persuade him at the death; so we hop into the jam and have it away over there very smartly. Giancarlo and Bill are there, who're always very loyal to me—also our waiter, Moishe, a dead old grafter: when you tell him grandly: 'Bring on the Krug, fellow,' he arrives with something my great-aunt Maria might have mixed up in her piss-pot and then holds smugly on to the change. So it is this time, but I give him one of my straight looks and we call it quits for trying and he brings me what we really want, which is gin. Mike belches loudly, but everyone in Winston's is so *loyal* that no one takes a blind bit of notice, except maybe trombone in the band who whimpers a little between his cloudy hair and cerulean dinner-jacket. It is deadly hot. . . . 'Oo, I'm going to get so bevvied I'll be like a lighthouse!'

'Good evening, dolling,' says a blowzy-looking hostess on my right—not one of the loyal ones.

'What's the matter?' says I. 'Your punter run out on you?'

'Never even got my present,' she mourns.

'Serves you right,' says I, 'for being so disloyal.'

'You're a little pouf,' says she, with a manic tiger grin. 'My steady'll see you tomorrow.'

'Any more of that,' says Mike on my left, breaking a tonic bottle, 'an I'll carve you so's you won't have any tomorrows.'

Charming.

At this point, though, there's a bit of dodgy clumping about behind, sound of birds scratching each other, things being knocked over and some larking about with pink curtains in front, and the cabaret comes poncing on.

'Look at all that bird!' says Mike, pouring a gin big as a lighthouse and scratching his barnet, while the first chorus comes on and springs dodgily about. I can see a pair of them fancying him more than *me*, which is a mild bit of aggravation. But the bird up there dances superbly because Winston's cabaret is no ordinary cabaret—the sort where a negro called Mr. Jaggers comes on really horsed and steps into a routine with a few cartwheels in which his top-hat doesn't fall off and then the compère comes on and drones: 'And now we take you over to gay Paree,' while the loyals throw fireballs about and search for birds' bristols to the accompaniment of low groans. No, here everyone dances like the hammers, because first a bloke comes on in tails and makes jokes and he's got it, the loyals, and the punters, right under the cosh and he really hits those punters packed densely in the scarlet room where they live, which is what they seem to like.

On come the birds again—as models this time. (Do you know? I've seen this *forty-two times* and I *still* love it?) I do fancy the bird in the front row second from left with the fabulous scotches—trouble is, though, she's a bit too young: once you've acquired a taste for the Stilton fruitiness of boilers it's a difficult thing to give up, so at the same time I can't help lamping an angry old creature dodging away like clockwork in the last row. Marchmare brought the first one I mentioned, Ginny-the-bird, to a party we gave the other day. Colonel Bulbul, our Nepalese business friend, fancied her like mad, but Marchmare had her away. As I said, Marchmare has all the luck with young bird. Still, the Archbubble and I had a typist from some spade Embassy one after the other, so in a way you can call it quits.

In the middle of this scene, vaguely uplifted, I turned to Mike and said: 'You know what, Mike? We're going to have a proper killing this time and make a bomb!'

'Think so?' he said to me, his eyes set sharp and half-shut—and I sensed at once that it wouldn't be for him; there was something in it that didn't fit; it wasn't *him*; I supposed then because he'd make a ton here and a pony there and live on the odd cock-and-hen between being in the nick—all down, I fancied, to that being his world, a sharp, hard, narrow world of a hard clout and an odd whore, same as he'd always known. It's not he was stupid: he was a deadly sharp deviator and intelligent, too, as you could see from the way he'd mixed into this deal, which wasn't exactly nishte, and then hung on and found us to help him—but he was used to grasses and that was where you had to be careful with people like Mike, to see he didn't try to work off on you all he'd had handed out to him—because most of the people he'd worked with were just lowdown grafting hoods who'd set him to work screwing—send him out with a pound of jelly, dets, or a dodgy twirl and then grass him to the law at the death so's to cut him out of his whack.

I look at him now and I can see he's thinking, which is something you must never never do, and he's looking a bit choked.

'You're looking a bit choked,' says I, and this leads on to another of his problems.

'Yes,' he says, 'it's down to glad.'

'Who's glad?'

'Glad's my girl.'

'What's up with glad your girl?'

'She's in the cat's-meat gaff havin' an ovary out.'

What *can* one say? 'That's not very loyal for her,' I says doubtfully, and I suppose I deserve a good clout for that because he whips round and snarls:

'No, it's not very loyal, it's not very *loyal*, is it?' and I don't know whether it's because he's bevvied up, but anyway he's got the dead needle.

'Don't go off so alarming,' I says.

After a minute off he says gloomily: 'Tell you what it is— only you probably wouldn't understand, being a stuck-up ponce and a Chelsea baron—it's all down to glad having to have it off with ice-creams all the time down to wages when she doesn't want it. You know what it is. Glad and me, we're caught up in this endless grind of her charvering an' me deviating, and she's not so young now, thirty-four. You don't know what it's like, havin' to go on the batter day in an' day out and havin' to open up for 'em all—big ones, thin ones, malts, spades, bubbles *and* the queans that beat 'er black an' blue. It's one thing when you're a kid of sixteen but glad, she's a big girl now. Mind, it wasn't like that all the time; time was when she 'ad a right little gaff an' she was the madam an' it was all down to beatin' punters or she'd get bird in from outside to take the wacks for a tenner. But then she got nicked for a carpet and when she got out, of course, the old clients 'ad all scarpered, you know how it is. *And* that's not all; just the other day she gets nicked along Piccy day before she's due to go in for cat's meat, an' under the new Act that's a pony and she's only got five more days to pay and I don't know where it's going to come from, morrie, and that's straight up and down I don't. *And* she's twenty-two carat, glad is; you should've seen how she used to come an' slip me snout when I was over at the ville.'

This is the sort of set-up where one's in danger of asking square questions, so I promptly asked one. 'You mean,' I said, 'you don't mind any old punter screwing your bird?'—and, sure enough, he turned on the calm, blank kind of butchers that people turn resignedly on to squares; and instead of answering he looked down, and slowly, almost *kindly*, crushed his glass and then dropped the bits and sat looking at his blood-covered hands while I sat marvelling through a cloud of vera and he said:

'It's all a fraud, I never wanted in on this deal. Some bearded old bastard dealt me in, put my loot on the cards, so I had to play. I'm going to tell *them* stupid bastard, stupid bastard, stupid bastard, and have a right old punch-up with the law and get nicked.'

'Have a care!' I cried feebly, but he got up by stages like one of those newsreels where you watch a horse lope in slow motion over the sticks, and went out without looking at me, gripping the heads of seated punters to steady himself.

Scarcely had I adjusted my boat to the look of gloom appropriate to a dodgy Hamlet playing with a shiv on the plaster-of-Paris battlements of Elsinore, though, when there was a loud cry near the door and the morries blundered in. Marchmare, grasping a passing hostess by the bottle, jumped happily up and down with her several times to suggest a scene sacred to Priap—which he did successfully enough to embarrass a dim, sticklike old person nearby, who sat sipping her Dubonnet with some others, hoping to pass unseen. The Archbubble was attempting to set fire to the edge of my table-cloth, whereas I had actually succeeded at it with the edge of his jacket:

' 'Tis Gapgrin and Slacktooth!'

Marchmare said into the ear of an ice-cream who sat monumentally suggesting a statue raised to The Unknown Punter: 'Secretary, how do I set about getting a bounder thrown out of the club?' while the Archbubble remarked: 'I want a table for one,' and sat down on my knees.

'Morrie,' says Marchmare to me, 'there's biz.'

'And biz here too,' I said fervently.

'Ah, but your biz isn't as good as our biz.'

'Bet you the jack-and-jill,' I snapped.

'Ow, do belt up and leave off,' growled the Archbubble.

More gin arrived and the glass was swept up and put on the bill.

'Our biz,' said Marchmare presently, 'is backing bent punters at one of Mrs. Byrd's dodgy spielers. What's yours?'

But when I told them, in a dead whisper lest Old Bill should have chosen this evening for a bevvy-up on the taxpayer, and flashed the beehive at them in the loo, you should have seen the way those morrie boats changed in a flash from innocent baby Greek giggles to glistening and intent earnestness.

'Are you on, then?' I said.

'On? Oi should effing well think so,' grumbled the Bubble; and Marchmare was speechless—he could only sit there nodding like a mandarin and burst into squeals of glee.

'Then—TO THE NORTH!' I screamed, against the battering strains of 'Blue Suède Shoes'.

'And now to dodgy chemmy,' said Marchmare at last, downing his vera.

'Yeeh,' growled the Archbubble—so Marchmare and I dived for the apples, leaving the Archbubble to moody and scream and go ahead over the jack-and-jill we'd left him with, and so ended this B minus scene at the plutocrattest joint on our manor.

I was in the loo when the bird from the cabaret passed me on her way to her loo to get the paint off her boat.

'Hullo,' she says with a wink.

'Watch the bristols!' I echo, soaking my boat, scrubbing it with a towel and combing the barnet.

'You morries up to your larks again?'

'Too right,' says I. 'Wish us luck.'

'Not on your nelly, mate,' she intones, 'do you *mind*!' and follows me with a catcall which assists me out of the gaff as neatly as if someone'd put a Roman candle under my bottle.

7

Out in the street I see, with much the same kind of shock that Villon would have got if he'd known he was going to see his boat in the *Sunday Times*, none other than valiant old Det. Sgt. Plinth!

In vain do I seek to stroll over to where the loyal commissionaire is holding my jam door very wide open for me—it is no good; the law has lamped me, so one must put a bold boat on things. Plinth is quite old, you know, really; and I think one of the reasons he dislikes us so much is that down to us he never gets a chance to go home to Hendon, get his boots off, slip into something loose and watch 'Dixon of Dock Green' on the telly—because there's always something brewing on the manor.

'Good evening,' says I airily, in the death, 'bit off your beat, isn't it?'

A gradual, dodgy sort of smile wanders diagonally through his whiskers and he teeters on his heels in a boxer-cum-butler kind of pose. . . . I don't know: sometimes I think it's high time they pensioned the old darling off and sometimes I go in dread of him as if he was Professor Moriarty and the Reichenbach Falls all rolled into one.

'Well,' he says, with that dreadful kind of affability the law puts on when it's trying not to be square ('Catch Your Deviator By Playing His Game': Week Two at the police college), 'off somewhere?'

'I should jolly well think so, Mr. Plinth,' says I. 'Off to bed.'
He lamps my kettle.

'That's a nice watch you've got.'

Really, nothing is sacred from the law—not even one's own personal bric-à-brac. What I'm dying to ask, of course, is if this is anything special, but of course one must never never do that, must one? So I play the old darling along.

'Yes, it is, isn't it?'

'Present from Dad, I dare say.'

Of course, it's nothing of the kind. It was koshered through London Airport inside the bra of a cosy old Swiss governess.

'Well, not exactly,' I said: 'it's just a sort of memento.'

'Ah,' he said. 'I see. Yes.'

A long pause.

'Well,' I said, 'I really must be getting along now. Early bed. Lots to do tomorrow, as usual.'

'Yes, I suppose you have,' says the legal old tearaway in undertaker's clothing, 'like a bit of rent-collecting up at Balls Pond Road, maybe?'

'Yes, well now, look,' I said, 'that's all perfectly kosher, you know. Anyway,' I added, in a flood of desperate invention, 'it's not that . . . rush off to Zürich . . . bird in Liechtenstein . . . Paris, dinner with an old boiler . . . Press . . . mustn't be seen here . . .' and I have a go at brushing imperiously by, but while the old devil doesn't exactly stop me he holds me with his Coleridge-like gaze and a dozen horrors flit across my mental scenery, though I know it's just a blag on his part really.

So I try the conversational, one-equal-to-another approach. 'Well,' I say, conscious of Bruce and all the boys in Winston's giggling a bit behind, 'how's the great world treating you? Eh? Crime and things O.K?'

'Oh, yes, they're OK.'

What *is* the old dear after? It gets more and more like Kafka every minute: I can quite see Plinth, come to think of it, as Klamm in *The Castle*.

'Yes,' I said helplessly, 'well, you simply must come round

and have a vera sometime' (the old darling isn't above it when things are peaceful) 'but now I really must be off.'

'After Mike, I suppose,' he said.

Yes, well now, there you are, you see. He must have tailed us in somehow. Don't ask me how he did it, dearie. But it just shows how you never quite know where you are with Old Bill. He's absolutely all about trout. Balls Pond Road first—no rent-collecting *there* tomorrow—and now this.

'Mike?' says I, looking mystified. 'I don't know what you mean. Really.'

Well, he gives me one of his straight looks while I manage to throw off a few of my jagged, innocent giggles; then, finally, the law relaxes.

'OK.,' he says, 'on your way now—and mind you don't drop too much loot you haven't got on them spielers of yours.'

I do my best to put on a boat of horrified outrage and as he turns away, striking the pavement with the dint of arméd heels, as Tennyson says, I hurry slowly (if you know what I mean) to the motor, from inside which I can see the pale boats of the morries gawping. Hop smartly into the seat, night-night and a dollar to the door-holding morrie and we're away out of it very much on the hurry-up.

'That looked dodgy,' said Marchmare.

'How right you are, darling,' I said. 'Did he have a word with you too?'

'Only same as he usually does: night-night, etc.'

'What was he doing up here, so far from home?' mused the Archbubble.

'Oh, just having an evening off and admiring the unique view along Clifford Street,' said I crossly—and then thoughtful silence till the dodgy spieler of Mrs. Byrd in Cad Square is reached.

8

I THINK a few words about this very grand bent spieler run by this strange old spade called Mrs. Byrd, and also a few about the way the morries work it, are now in order. While we are standing on the stagey doorstep, having just announced ourselves through the speaking-box affair, it is not hard for us to picture what sort of dialogue, to the nearest lighthouse, is proceeding between our gracious hostess and her tame heavy inside. But we know, in our infinite wisdom, what the outcome will be. Though she would dearly like not to, Mrs. Byrd will in fact let us in.

Her reluctance stems chiefly from the morries' fierce and primitive method of playing chemmy. Not being a cash game but a credit one, if we lose we knock. Secondly, we never somehow *do* lose—and anyone can see what bad biz this is for Mrs. Byrd, since reddies which should be sailing into her African kick are instead diverted to ours and zoom into them like drones conforming on a quean bee in spring weather. The reason why morries never lose at bent spielers is, naturally, *because* they're bent; all the bent grafters prefer to play along with us rather than Mrs. Byrd—for the simple reason that we *pay* much better. Mrs. Byrd, in fact, choked though she would be to know it, is regarded in the trade as little more than African mutton dressed up as Canterbury lamb: one of those poor old boilers who think: 'Hello, here's an easy way to make some loot,' and promptly does her lot. So you see, if you *know*

all the bent punters who are supposed to be bending the game
pour la maison, and then you get them to play along with you
instead of the *maison*, getting wages is about as simple as getting
a charver in the kasbah when you've got half a ton on you. See?
And thus it follows that, provided one simply backs the bent
player and gets one's punter to back the player who *isn't* bent
with large private bets away from the table, one neatly drains
all the punters' loot off into one's bin before it ever *gets* to the
table—and one leaves after the modest hour or so dragging
away a great sack of wages from under Mrs. Byrd's distracted
nose . . . and you can see how Mrs. Byrd would operate her
game far more profitably if no morries were there. But there
are heavy reasons why Mrs. Byrd cannot leave us to the mercy
of the London night like babes in the wood, or have her tearaway thump us over the lump with a cosh. This is because we
can draw on more strength to come and break up Mrs. Byrd's
game than Mrs. Byrd, to put it crudely, has had hot dinners:
the stoutest heart would quail at seeing, for instance, the entire
contents of the Tealeaf marching up the steps of that grandiose
but illegal gaff to bang impressively for admittance—loud
enough, in fact, to attract the attention of that ever-dodgy
spectre, Old Bill. So, on the whole, we are always granted
admission sooner than fast. In a rather naked way, it's not
unlike the City or any other old place where loot is made
legit—bent or straight, the basic tactics of pressure neatly
applied are much the same; underneath the frock coat and
whiskers the making of loot and wages is never a pretty sight
—and thus the aggressive female spade (who launched her
game auspiciously with the twin gimmicks of wearing spade
national dress with a wishbone through her nose and having
a cash float of *three grand*, poor old darling) has no spur with
which to prick the sides of her intent but vaulting financial
ambition, as the great man says, which, when the morries
arrive, unfortunately o'erleaps itself and falls on the other.

Anyway, I hope I have now made it well and truly plain why
Mrs. Byrd's Afrique knickers are well and truly round her

ankles and why she is properly over a Greek barrel, and why we are admitted to the august presence after a wait of perhaps ten seconds.

So in we buzz, one, two, three: peck the dusky old boiler (all except the Archbubble who suddenly gets a fit of the trembling fancies and hugs her nearly to death) and scan the drum. This is exceedingly large, and the chemmy table, though large too, fills only a corner of it.

All is a low mutter and hum of brains and eyes clocking and working out how soon to knock, and the weary, ponderous instructions of the croupier under the shaded lights knocked for from Lillywhite's.

Clocking around myself, it seems to me that Mrs. Byrd must have put a great deal of thought into organizing this particular game, because the gaff (well furnished, restrained and at first sight not unlike a morrie's) is crawling with punters; so many, in fact, that there isn't enough room for them all to play, which of course is how the morries get their foot in. So a lot of ice-creams are standing about getting bevvied on Mrs. Byrd. *But* out of this maelstrom of punters, like a sore thumb on a hand, sticks up a figure.

A grafter is hard at work.

I creep up unseen, and above the general rabbiting discern the sweetest tones of Oxford. . . . Why! 'tis darling, *chubby*, NORTH-WEST FRONTIER Colonel Bulbul, our Nepalese business friend, raising his delicate Sikh-like lip in a fubbsy smile to reveal the pearliest of teeth, and I hear the mesmeric voice saying: ' . . . And so, if I can get away to Stockholm first thing tomorrow, old fellow, I don't see why the first cargo of fifty-three thousand machine-guns shouldn't reach Bogotá by way of Montevideo tomorrow week.'

(Cardboard machine-guns, of course.)

'My God, Krishna,' says Bathwarpe, the pink, boiled-looking solicitor who sits before Bulbul in a half-crouch, 'that's pretty fast work, isn't it?'

'Yes, yes,' says Bulbul in a terribly tired whisper, passing a hand rapidly over his black immaculate barnet and yawning to show his dusky little tonsils. 'Ah, but you don't know how I've been rushing about like a *lunatic* over it.'

'So of course,' says Bathwarpe in a rush, 'you'll want the first cheque now, won't you?'

'Yes, yes; ten thousand, please,' says Bulbul, looking the other way, 'and make it cash—I'll have to discount it . . . never do to use the big five when the revolution's only a week off.'

'No, no, Bulbul,' says the punter anxiously, 'for God's sake don't do that.' But then, wavering: 'Ten thousand? It's going to play the very dickens with my overdraft.'

But Bulbul only gave him one of those lovely conspiratorial smiles that's been the envy of every con man since God was a tiny boy, and patted Bathwarpe soothingly on the arm as the latter wrote his kite on the mantelpiece. 'Don't worry, old fellow,' he said softly and caressingly, magnetizing him with those gleaming eyes, 'you're going to make such a killing a fortnight from today that you'll never have a financial worry again in your life!'

'Just as well,' I heard the punter mutter, 'I don't know what the senior partner's going to say as it is.'

Bulbul swung round at this moment and saw me, standing entranced as I drank up the foregoing in silent admiration.

'Well?' he snapped, 'what did Garcia say?'

I caught on. 'Paulo's all right,' I said anxiously, 'at least, I think so.' I could see Bathwarpe standing there watching us with a cunning look and I nearly spoiled it all by giggling. But I sank my voice to a whisper which Bathwarpe could just hear: 'And Bienvenida's evidently decided not to attack the palace, thanks to the referendum on Wednesday.'

'Phew!' breathes Bulbul softly, 'thank God. Anything from the office?'

'Yes,' I said. 'I had to sell Brasilia Destructives.'

'What at?' said Bulbul, with darling, fubbsy anger.

'Hundred and seven-eighths,' I said mournfully. 'It was all I could get.'

Bulbul's face distorted with rage and despair. 'You fool,' he groaned, 'oh, you *fool*! I told you to hang on till Monday no matter what Wall Street did. Can't I turn my back for a *second*?'

'But Garcia——' I began.

'Oh, damn and blast the fellow Garcia!' said Bulbul.

I was introduced to Bathwarpe.

'Who is this Garcia?' he wanted to know.

'The absurd Garcia,' said Bulbul, 'is'—pointing to me—'his business manager in—well, we know where, Bathwarpe.'

'Ah, yes; yes, I see,' said Bathwarpe, as Bulbul neatly slipped the written kite out of his hand.

'And you will expel him,' said Bulbul, who too often thought of later life in terms of schools in Pondicherry.

'I will,' I said.

Bulbul looked bored for a minute. Then he pulled a vast wad of beehives—about a monkey—from an inner pocket.

'I shall play this for a minute, old fellow,' he said, 'while you entertain my associate.'

And with that he made his way to the table near which Marchmare and the Archbubble were taking the private bets—altogether the neatest climax to a piece of graft I've seen.

Bathwarpe and I wandered over to the chemmy table.

'Funny little game, isn't it?' I said casually.

'Yes, yes, isn't it?' said the half-wide mug. 'I say, I can't tell you how excited I am about this deal with Bulbul—I suppose it's all right to talk to you about it as you work for him?'

'Yes, yes,' I said testily. I was bored with cardboard machine-guns. I hadn't covered myself for wages yet. I took a quick lamp over the baize, where butter was busy melting in every mouth but two; where it was not melting was in the mouths of the dodgy punters, sitting at numbers one and six. Six was now playing, running his bank for the third time, the bent croupier looking understandably bored. So I quickly chipped in with Bathwarpe.

'Quick!' I said. 'Bet a pony the box. There's just time.'

'You're on,' he said, downing one of Mrs. Byrd's sizzling scotches.

'Forty-nine pound ten in the bank,' intoned the croupier listlessly.

A sharp knock from number eight. 'Banco,' he said.

'Prime,' said number four crossly.

'Prime is called,' said the croupier, and the cards went to number four, who duly lost. I paid in reddy, slapped Bathwarpe on the back and took him off for another drink.

Someone got up and went off rather sad-looking with a pocket like an empty windsock. Colonel Bulbul, who had been waiting uneasily behind everyone's chairs for this to happen, slipped into the departed's place.

We did eye eggy-peggy.

Bent! shouted mine.

I know! his said.

Then why? mine simply screamed.

C'est pour le frisson, replied his languidly, with a perfect French accent, so I gave up and rejoined my punter, watching the morries who were cleaning up nicely too, but I reckoned I'd done better than they had, having it away with Bathwarpe.

I waited twenty minutes and then wandered back again. Sure enough, number six was just taking the bank again.

He put in a beehive.

'Banco,' said someone.

'Double that pony I lost to you?' I said. Somehow it never seemed to occur to him I might have lost it on purpose.

'You're on,' he croaked. I wondered if later I might not switch a bird on to him to finish him right up.

Cards.

Bank has seven.

'Stands,' intones the croupier. 'Card?'

'Yeeh,' says the punter, who used to run a dodgy spieler of his own before he went into antiques on the proceeds back in the days before the morries fixed it. He gets a four to nothing.

'And the bank wins. Ten pounds in the bank.'

'Banco prime . . .'

'Double or quits?' I murmur.

'No, but I'd like that other pony.'

Yellow streak down his back!

'*Neuf à la banque!*'

'That's fifty,' says I. 'Still game?'

'Of course!' says Bathwarpe crossly, downing another Scotch. 'In fact'—looking at me roguishly—'double or quits.'

'After all,' I murmur, 'why should you care? You'll be as rich as Croesus by the end of the month . . . and look at Bulbul —doing a bomb.'

As indeed he was.

The bank won again, as it had to; and now, out of the corner of my eye, I see darling Ginny-the-bird from Winston's cabaret approaching on my right, just who I've been waiting for, so I give her the hi-sign and she comes up and hangs on to Bathwarpe's arm—poor bastard, about forty he is and I can see him fancying her like mad, and he's that poor sort of creep who's got to play so that his winnings can give him the *empressement* he'd never otherwise have with bird. So now I catch the croupier's eye and eyesay to him to switch it so that the bank loses on the next coup. It's the end of the show and for answer he just bends down very deep as he starts in on the *salade*, which means everything's jake.

'So that's a ton down you are,' says I to Bathwarpe, non-chalantly. And this is where you have to be careful with the blag. 'You didn't have much luck with the box last time,' I says meaningfully, as if I were up to something, 'so if you have it again this time you'll probably win.'

He gives me that I-know-thee-for-what-thou-art look, as I knew he would, and says: 'No, I'll play it the other way for a change,' which was just how I had it fixed with the croupier.

'Oh, all right,' I says, eyes gleaming, the poor soak, 'let's say double or quits again.'

'Right you are.'

Bathwarpe pays up by kite, which I discount for cash with

Bulbul in the loo and also collect a pony for my inventive flights over 'Garcia', so I have it away back to the gaff a right few quid ahead . . . and we'll have a few laughs over lunch tomorrow in the Tealeaf when I give the croupier his cut and Ginny-the-bird comes in to squawk over how much she hit Bathwarpe for afterwards and pay us *our* whack too, I wouldn't wonder, for steering her in.

9

Yes, this slush operation is big time. One minute we were still teamed up at the off-line, but then Mike reported to say he'd phoned Reisemann and Reisemann said it was on, and that had the effect of pressing that red button marked 'Fire', and we're bolting through the cloud once more into the stratosphere of big-time deviation where nothing's certain any more and I look back for the safe, cosy ways of making small-time wages like I've just been on about, or even for the slag, but it's just a pigmy globe swinging about way back there, and I'm afraid and I don't care who knows it, because I never knew anyone who played for a quarter of a million stake who didn't come across a big bolted door somewhere en route with the word 'Trouble' on it.

I suppose we all get these bad moments: the cold, sweating palms, the tingling hysteria and its forced suppression, and the feeling it's a dream, and then putting one's hand into one's pocket and feeling the car tickets for the air ferry and the tight packs of foreign currency and knowing its hard fact. Then, to telescope all that time between today and the day you're going, you feel like copping for the blower and dialling any old bird for kicks. In fact, all the tensions which together compose the sweet thrill of fear whose orgasm is coolness and a fast-talking tongue in time of trouble.

Outside in Rome Street it is pouring with sudden rain and it's dark green, so I go to the double windows and open them, and, though I smoke too much, I stand in the first-floor drawing-room and smell the air between me and the low grey sky as though I'd never smelled it, and sense the whole house behind me, empty and listening. It's a meaningful silence, like the tape-recorders in Spain all over again. That day I was queuing up for a third-class ticket to La Granja, knowing there were two Seguridad men paring their nails absently in the sunny, deserted station; I was very lucky that time.

It's no good: I can't stand there just looking and thinking, the thing you must never do. So I go back and stick on a pop record. Waiting for the disc to fall and the needle to swing, I feel in my pocket and bring out a darling little snuff-box which I keep my snap in. I crack the ampoule and breathe in *hard* just as the first chord of the guitar strikes the room and the sick voice of the singer hits an electronic B flat while my head pops and crackles and swells and floats off like a balloon from the snap, and then the phone rings.

'Flaxman 31018.'

'Morrie?'

'Morrie!'

It is Marchmare.

'I'm full of snap, morrie!'

'Where going?'

I decide. 'Navarre Crescent. Christice's basement.'

'May see you there.'

Rings off. But off I bound, feeling a heap better—into the jam to Lord and Lady Chrism's house in Navarre Crescent: brake-screech and hurtle out of the jam and look at the basement and it's full of slag . . . its bottoms all ranged along the sill under the open window. Smoke and bang and chatter of glasses. No time to explain about Christice now. Only one thing to do about all that slag—there's a brick there, so I pick it up and hurl. Bang through the window. No slag hit, but all *smothered* in glass, and that followed by two fireballs flung with the master's hand and lo! sylphidewise one falls with a dying fall flop almost on to a bird's espresso-bongo hairdo. And so enter with yet another triumph over our deadliest enemy the slag.

Mixed applause and irritation.

'Darling.'

'Oh, it's that dreadful person.'

'Darling.'

'Christice.'

For I have seen her.

'Not X about the window?'

' 'Course not.' (Oh, yes, I shall *have* to explain about Christice but there isn't *time*.)

'Have snap?'

' 'Course. Have snap will travel.'

A person in twill trousers and black winklepickers turns to Christice, saying above my immoderate hoots of laughter:

'Marry me.'

And Christice turns to him and replies sincerely: 'But with what object in *view*?'

He goes, who knows where, and we take snap, and get snapped up, and now snap nearly *does* knock our blox off. We gaze at each other mothily, with idiotic smiles.

I put my arm round her. Christice violently loyal.

'I only see you every three months,' she mourns.

'Ah, I know,' I said, following an interior snap train, 'but keeping things too long makes them warp and disappear, and that would never do.'

But she is not listening.

'We must have a lovely party.'

'Where are nasty Lord and Lady Chrism?'

'Away,' she breathes. 'For two days, isn't it wonderful?'

'And now for a drink,' I say, and this procured we rush about the basement like two toppling lighthouses, snapped to the skies. But at last, like a roulette ball, I settle into a slot. Opposite me I find a dark slag.

'I write books,' he says, with no preamble. It is the one who asked Christice to marry him. Do you *mind*!

'Not I,' I said gravely.

'No, no, not you, *I*,' he corrects crossly. 'And you?'

''Cause books to be written,' I say loftily.

'Aha, aha, yes,' he laughs nastily, wagging his beaker at me. 'I know you.'

'Charming,' says I coldly, moving off.

No lights, the afternoon turning dark suddenly, so it must be evening, the slag thinning, the place still bulging with smoke and river ooze, and I, glacial snows melting: 'Christice!'—and draw her down to the floor: Christice, large and profound—oh, a deep one, those Wedgwood eyes!—sitting with me on the floor like a small girl still sitting on the heather somewhere on some awful August day in Scotland or Ireland, with Lord Chrism out rooting with the guns staggering like lead soldiers across a bleak horizon and little funny brown birds whizzing round their heads like sparrows, and pop, pop—nice shot, my lord—and now old, and Christice, on the bottle and snap *and* a bit of a leaper bedwise, hopeless in a different way.

'What are you thinking about?' she says.

'Nothing,' says I, feeling in my pocket for more snap, 'that couldn't be well expressed in a hatful of tennis-balls,' and then my hand, still, as it always did, of its own accord, was narrowly and eagerly struggling in the thicket of Virid Dresses round her thighs; and she looks downwards to me, and luscious AND . . . *así que pásen cuatro anos.*

'But we were too clever for each other in those days,' she says, snatching at this inward diary of my thoughts.

'No, no,' I said.

'But you're so nasty nowadays.'

'No, no, *no*!'

'But you *are*.'

How can I explain to her everything I've said so far? And it would mean thinking, and that one must never *never* . . . out with the snap-box. Moody silence broken by the thoughtful popping of ampoules and Christice aiming hers at the last slag who won't go, and 'I wish he'd *go*' she says as it hits him—

and there! it's like visiting one's little cousin in the country when one was a child, at an airless house with too many clipped ducks quacking on the quaint lake. . . . I *will* explain about Christice: but meanwhile is it to be a stalemate? Never a play-off? Or just sex, ended with the night—though *that's* final enough: I'd rather be dead. We, Christice and I, the on-and-on of life, its stuff and energy—everything goes boom as you touch it, a white bloom and flash, quick as the blast of snap. Christice knows: sex, that's nothing; you just have it and then it's over. Attraction? That could run you over out of the blue, like a bus. Christice isn't like Mrs. Marengo; there are hundreds of Mrs. Marengos, but there's only one Christice. When we make love we do it gently, somehow, almost kindly, a rare thing in our lives, that. Then if sex was out of the way you could *talk*. With Mrs. Marengo I'm just a ponce. Only, even ponces live with their women. But, after all, that's just economics with them, isn't it?

'What are you doing nowadays?' says Christice. The slag has gone, and she is throwing bottle-tops at the wall.

'Biz. Off to krautland in a day or two.'

'Well, come back safe.'

'You should care,' says I.

'Oh, how *silly* you are to say a thing like that. You must be potty.'

'I am potty,' I say. 'Believe me. I absolutely am.'

'All right. I believe you,' she says sourly.

'More snap, darling?'

'O.K., I don't mind. . . . How's Tumbledown Towers?'

That's my name for the house where my parents live.

'Oh, it's all right. . . . By the way, Marchmare's meant to be coming.'

'He won't come. I don't like Marchmare. I don't fancy him, even.'

'He doesn't fancy you, either.'

'*I* don't care.'

'He thinks you're an old bag.'

'I don't care if he does think I'm an old bag.'

'You're not, though.'

'But I was rather when I was having my Cure, wasn't I?'

'Yes, you were then. But I didn't mind you, just the same.'

'No, I know. You were sweet then.'

'There's nothing very sweet about me,' I said. 'You ought to realize that by now.'

'There is really. You just don't quite understand about things.'

'I wish we could go to Greece together one day.'

'Well, we will one day. You wait and see.'

'I wish it was now,' I said, feeling restless.

'Love me?' she said.

'You know I do,' I said.

'I love you,' she said; 'it's so easy to love you.'

'I love you, I love you, I love you, I love you.'

'A rose is a rose is a rose is a rose.'

'Kiss kiss.'

'M-m-m-m-m.'

'Slag's gone.'

'Good,' I said. 'I'm not going.'

'Good,' she said. 'That means we can beat it loyally upstairs to Mummy's room. Down here's too squalid.'

'Goodness, how strange,' I said. 'It seems ages and ages ago since last time.'

'Yes, isn't it funny?'

'Yes and we had a row.'

'And you cried.'

'Yes, because we thought one had to be *loyal* and do the decent thing and buy a Ring.'

We went upstairs.

'Why,' I said, 'your breasts have gone all funny since the last time I saw them.'

'They've just got bigger, that's all. I think it must be the drink.'

'No, it's not just that—they sort of whirl about like those torpedo things you see at the funfair.'

'No, they *don't*.'

'Well, they do a bit. Have some snap. It makes you love like mad.'

'I shan't need much incentive to do that.'

'Nor me. Still, you might as well have some.'

'I'm not supposed to. All those sort of things are supposed to be on the index for me.'

'Well, in that case you simply *must* have some, mustn't you?'

'I suppose so, yes.'

More popping of ampoules.

'I can't get this horrible *thing* off,' she said, wrestling with her girdle.

'Well, leave it on, then.'

'All right. . . . I say, snap is *funny*, isn't it? It's like oxygen or something all white and your heart goes like a *lunatic*.'

'With three screws after him.'

'Hiding in a wood.'

'Of shame.'

'Oh, naturally. You don't write any more poetry, do you?'

'No. Lie down here.'

'I said *you don't write any more poetry*.'

'No, I'm too big for that now. Lie down here.'

'Love's so loyal with you. Because you're so loyal.'

'You've got the lines mixed. I'm supposed to say that.'

'Well, you were too late. I say, you will come back safe, won't you?'

'Of course I will. Why ever not?'

'Well, because you never know. Chelsea's so disloyal. I don't care what else you do but just come back.'

'Darling, darling Christice, you are so loyal.'

'So are you. Now don't talk any more.'

'All right.'

10

'I WONDER what it is we must deplore, that turned us into morries evermore?' I was humming under my breath as I drove smartly along Chelsea Embankment to pick up Christice. I don't know: what just happened between me and her made me want to see her again; she was good for my nerves, which were bad, as they always are just before the off, and I needed her because I didn't have to think with her: she was the clean spot in the sludge. And when she gave me everything she had she gave me *back* something—which no other bird ever did. And I was depressed besides because the agent for Rome Street had just paid us another nasty visit and it was becoming evident, even to Marchmare, that we couldn't go on knocking there much longer—and the interval between gaffs is always so drab, isn't it?

Well, now I'll release a bit more about Christice, as I've been meaning to. I've known Christice for five years, off and on, not that that seems to bring a solution to the muddle any closer. Though her dad's a lord, she's none too well fixed for the dot-and-dash, and somehow it goes against the grain *not* to be seen around with an heiress—if only on account of the slag, who think of nothing else. (Funny, everyone seems to care about what *someone* else thinks—even if it's only the slag. We seem to be engaged in this dreadful battle of one-upness with the slag, even though we *have* been taught to dress properly and say thank you nicely when the horrid sticky cakes come round.)

In the trade, then, she's known as Lady Christice; and her parents, like mine, drop into the slot which I label with a word of my own, because the kosher dictionaries haven't got round to thinking of one yet. They're pompoons: that's to say, if you say retrench-and-reform-oh-for-an-hour-of-Gladstone very quickly they can hardly resist coming to with a start and saying: 'Oh, *heavens*, yes.' Unfortunately, though, five years ago I was younger and greener, and instead of saying all that first I couldn't wait and eloped with Christice the very first time we met, the morning after she'd smuggled me over the back hedge by the swimming-pool into a deb dance at Hurlingham. We were gone only three weeks, but do you know? you'd have thought the banks had shut down, the screaming and going ahead that went on. And when fubbsy old Lord Chrism finally picked us up, broke, on Battersea Bridge in a hired Ford Anglia, I found myself on the barred list.

I suppose I wasn't much catch for a son-in-law—not least because I didn't have anything like that in mind—and though Christice tells me the old dear is sadder and wiser now that he's met some of her subsequent boy friends (one of the Soho ones picked his teeth with a match the whole way through dinner, I'd have given a fortune to see *that*), it doesn't help much when it comes to me picking her up at the Chrism gaff in Navarre Crescent. Even my handwriting's known and they pinched both the letters I ever wrote her—one was from Spain when I needed a few exes to help with the tape-recorders—and I'd like to have watched their boats when they read *that* one too. No go on the blower either: they know my dulcet tones, but all that heavy breathing on the nursery extension shows what amateurs they are.

However, I go and pick her up on the front doorstep just the same; on purpose, really, to listen in on the angst going on indoors when I arrive.

Christice is marvellous, because she doesn't care what people think—not at the time, that is. That it catches up on her after-wards shows in the way she gets so bevvied for days at a time, moodying round Soho in jeans, carrying a wicker basket full of knitting and unread copies of the *Statesman* and a blotchy old handbag . . . also the Cure, which was down to mental angst as much as the river ooze, really.

And, you know, when she's had a couple of nights' sleep and takes a bit of trouble with her boat and getting her stockings on straight she looks twenty-two carat—enough to make you catch your breath when you're dancing with her and wish things were different.

So I screech to a stop in front of the Chrism London residence in Navarre Crescent—as nice a bit of keep-yourself-to-your-self Chelsea brickwork, gangling and blushing like a hideous old schoolboy, as you could wish to pop on the property market.

But there are those four brothers.

Nimbly, I scramble from the jam and press all three bells. A long delay: then Christice gallops slowly downstairs. As she opens the door a crack it's just like boy meets girl across the river.

'Oh, it's you,' she breathes. 'I thought it was a writ.'

Yes, well I know she's got that breathing voice, only it's not that *dreadful* breathiness the scrubbers put on in the Cavalry-man; their espresso-bongo hairdos deceive no one, while Christice's is all set to slaughter the crowd, half of it hanging down one shoulder . . . *she* doesn't care.

'Well, come in, come in,' she says irritably, clocking up and down the street all about trout, 'I don't want the neighbours to see you.'

'Well,' I said, 'after that slaggy basement of yours that will be a treat for me, coming upstairs.'

'Yes,' she says joyfully, '*they're* out till late, and there's a full quart of vodka I haven't touched waiting for you *and* all the new steel-band discs you'll love . . . so we can get perfectly drunk before we need even think about dinner.'

'Vodka!' I shout, plunging upstairs after her. 'To the *North*!'

And that's the effect Christice has on me: she makes me forget all about morries and deviation and poker and we turn into a couple of schoolkids. Emerging into the Chrism drawing-room on the first floor: goodness! I'd quite forgotten what it looked like—very kosher and *much* airier and bigger than I remembered it; the last time I suppose the whole place was too cluttered up with the angst flying about and Lady Chrism turning the taps on and Christice twisting out of Lord Chrism's grasp and pelting with me down to Oakley Street and us catching a 49 bus and going round and round talking because there was nowhere else left to talk in and we were shickered.

So now we hug each other in the middle of the floor and she gives me a monster wet kiss and her bra strap breaks and while she's fixing it I turn and see two of those Waterford glasses and the immense bottle of vodka. Then we rush upstairs and pinch her brother's portable gramophone and in no time at all the whole room is screaming with Elias and his Zigzag Jive Flutes and we've downed three vodka-and-tonics before we can draw breath; and outside it's a fine green, green summer's evening and the flags of the trees wave slowly in front of the river that makes a mirror sparkling behind them; and then, furrowing through Christice's records, what should I find but one disc we bought together years ago: Mezzrow's Revolutionary Blues with de Paris blowing fit to burst and we play it three times and then slowly, slowly, we begin to feel drunk—right there while it's broad daylight still; and we clasp each other and circle round the room, and Lord Chrism the Forty-First looks down the end of his beak at us and the sun sets right over the first-floor balcony.

And with this music there's no question of sitting down to listen to it like the squares do—or lying down on a sofa or bed and letting one's hair drip down and thinking goodness aren't I dissolute and pretending to play cards, which is what the slag do.

Christice and I can't sit still for a minute.

'We must have some more loyals in!'

'But where are they?'

'I know where there must be some,' says I.

I go out on to the balcony, and, sure enough, there is some-one down there in the street, full length on his tummy and half invisible under an old motor.

'Hey, you!' I scream. Christice added her crazy trills.

It takes quite a time for the penny to drop, but finally the person scrambles up, all over oil.

'Poor *darling*,' says Christice. Then raising her voice to full scream from the balcony: 'Come up and have a drink!'

The poor bird stands swaying in the street, oil running off his hands: he is quite red in the boat and his mouth is slightly open, as if he'd that second been shot.

'Oh, I couldn't,' he said.

'Why couldn't you?' coos Christice.

'Oo, well, because I couldn't,' murmurs he.

'Here,' I said, 'I'll nip down and talk to the ice-cream.'

'Yes, do,' said Christice imploringly. 'You know,' she added in an undertone, 'I think I quite fancy him.'

So I descend to street level to have a rabbit with him. You know, it's extraordinary the effect it has on people if you go straight up to them and tell them they're loyal. Unless they're very square, a hundred to one it works: you arrest them with a new thought, plunging suddenly from the blue. So with this person, dressed in an old sports coat and pre-war Oxford bags, sparse hair sticking up on top and red in the boat and in fact thoroughly *loyal*.

I tugged him by the arm. 'Come on,' I said strictly. 'Upstairs. Christice wants to see you.'

'Christice?' he said dimly. I think he believed he was dreaming.

'Ooh,' he said. 'I couldn't possibly.' He was quite old; about forty.

'Yes, yes,' I said crisply. 'One drink. Just one. Then you can

84

explain why you can't have it while you're actually having it. A new experience.'

'You're joking,' he said.

'I'm certainly *not*,' I said, firmly repressing the idea of finding out if he was a punter. 'These things happen. It *has* happened.'

Christice stood on the balcony, cooing down at him.

'All right,' he muttered. 'Just one.'

And he was halfway upstairs while he said it.

'Really,' he said faintly, 'I'm simply not fit . . . to be seen. . . . I must go and clean up before I . . .'

'Ridiculous,' said Christice distinctly from the drawing-room, 'you'll come exactly as you are and no more fuss. It's only me after all,' she added illogically.

I could see her from the stairs, squatting down sexily and turning the discs over.

So, leading him in dazed, we placed our totem, after some discussion as to where he would look best, in front of the fire-place and put a huge vodka in his hand. He had at it in gasps, sucking it down, I think in relief it was all no worse, as if he'd flown up there, which of course he had in a way.

Christice pressed the button and more steel-band jazz began bouncing off the venetian mirrors.

'What's your name?' shouted Christice above the beat of these engines.

'Jim!' he shouted back. Now his dim face was all crooked and aglow with a new excitement and astonishment, his rucked hair standing straight up and his eyes saucer-round and quite foolish with fun and he was laughing.

'What do you do?' I asked him curiously.

He *was* forty and lived alone with his mother up the street.

'I work in an income-tax office,' he said. 'I'm an inspector of taxes.' He shouted it out like one revolutionary soldier to another, aflame with new ideas in a trench during an attack. Our astonishment was enormous and mutual: Christice and I had never met people quite like him before; not head-on, I mean. He was unquestionably *loyal*: I couldn't define the word better

85

than by applying it to that situation, composed by scooping one half of it straight off a London street and popping it into the other half—the house of the absent arch enemy, the pompoons and squares, which we were busy defiling with our laughter, hurling down the almighty which had so often tried to propel us with its irrevocable orders, its finger stiffly pointed in absurd directions like those painted fingers which tell you the way to the loo in stations and zoos.

'Well, well,' said Christice, 'drink up—there isn't a moment to lose'—and indeed there wasn't: you could feel time rushing under you like a moving staircase your feet didn't quite touch. It was blind and uncaring, was time, taking you on to new time whether you liked it or not. Christice started dancing with Jim. A moment before he would have protested, but he was now initiated; it had accomplished a lot, that moment. Christice put her cheek to his, and he seemed to fill out like a balloon, as if his astonishment were some kind of gas, and to want to float off; and he stopped dancing as he had at the beginning, like an assistant bank manager at Bricktops his first night out in Rome, or a determined deb's escort hopping dutifully to a foxtrot amid the swinging necklaces and bead bags: now he rocked with a furious devoted energy; and when Christice's face came away from his cheek she was all smeared with oil and as he danced her up and down you could hear spare bits of his old motor clanking in his pockets.

But at last he had to go and cook his mother's dinner. We begged him to cop for the blower and tell her he'd be late, but he began to wring his hands and display a pitiable anguish: 'I must go, I *must*,' he said earnestly—so Christice let him go and he at once darted off as rapidly as he had come, like the White Rabbit, popping and bobbing a moment, dutifully saying thank you in the doorway. It was pitiful to see him surging back into his nameless sea of income tax and anonymity: I could have cried.

If anyone had asked me what I wanted to take with me to a desert island, like they do in that funny S-man programme on the B.B.C., of course I'd have said Christice without hardly thinking. Yet the odd thing is that we spend as much time far from each other as near. I don't know what it is: I suppose life intervenes, or Mrs. Marengo; or suddenly you wake up and it's a fine morning and nothing will do but you must rush off to Spain and have another try at the tape-recorders, or it's some other kind of deviation—or else we have a row—just a meaningless, sudden one, and we get drunk somewhere on a reconciliation kick and I look round and she's gone off. Don't ask me how, but the man she's talking to somehow gets stuck to her in some particular minute and he's part of the minute, and so sex seems the natural thing, with no *arrière pensée*. But we always end up together again somehow.

It seems to me that no matter whether you marry, settle down or live with a bird or not, certain ones simply have your number on them, like bombs in the war; and even if you don't happen to like them all that much there's nothing you can do about it—unless you're prepared to spend a lifetime arguing fate out of existence, which you could probably do if you tried but I'm not the type.

I was thinking all this as Christice and I sat opposite each other at the Trois Assommeurs, noshing. The Trois Assommeurs is a very loyal place—if you don't mind the expense, which I don't. As a matter of fact, I'm fond of expensive places for their own sake. After all, look at it this way. I spend my time fleecing the half-wide mugs, don't I? Do I resent restaurants for doing the same to me? Hell, of *course* I don't. Fact is, it'd make me feel very uncomfortable if they didn't. Mind, that's provided the gaff's a loyal one where the waiters don't all look at you as if you were Louis XVI having his elevenses. That's the sort of place where I go in simply because I happen to be hungry, need a kosher meal and am skint. I go in *meaning* to knock. But places like Winston's and the Trois Assommeurs it'd be a *crime* to knock, because the nosh is a wicked price on purpose to keep the slag out, and because everyone's so loyal in there. But you've got to distinguish between us and the slag here: us who knock a place because the people are nasty, and the slag who knock because they're so stupid they think it's the Done Thing. It must be extraordinary to be as stupid as that, mustn't it, but my word they manage it.

'How are you off for cash?' said Christice, breaking in on these important thoughts. It was nice the way she said cash like a civilized girl and not reddies or something: though she was in the morrie world she was somehow not quite of it, which made me fonder of her than almost anything else—when I say Christice was *loyal* I mean she had values of some kind, though daughter to pompoons. Nothing strikes me worse than slag bird where, of course, by definition, things are quite the opposite.

Though it was a summer's night, Christice was wearing her Russian fur cap. She'd bought it in *Russia* too, not Knightsbridge; she went there on a grinding trip with her brother-in-law in a Dormobile. But Christice is very tough—a hereditary toughness, which is, I dare say, handed down through pompoon families like ours and may be a faint excuse for their existence, though not necessarily their survival. Looking at her, I was impressed anew by how true it was that she and I represented the crust on its *very* uppers. We had both been to the best schools; Christice had even been presented at court, because when she refused poor Lady Chrism threw such a fit that Christice took pity on her wasting away like that among half-empty Chanel bottles and the two Orpens in her bedroom and said all right ... and then me, dodging about Chelsea with my dreadful chat and getting in the linens all the time down to larking and tangling with Old Bill and going to the Tealeaf every day and mixing with straight deviators and having a sus file at the Yard. And yet, looking at her again, I remembered my favourite photograph of her at Navarre Crescent which I should have so much liked to have but couldn't ask for somehow: a girl of eleven with her hair blowing in the wind, sitting in the tall grass somewhere or other in the country with a sly look on her boat. Yes, with Christice this evening things were way above the high-water mark and thanks to her there was no need to think, something you must never never. . . . I reached into my bin and pulled out sixty quid (oh, yes, because I'd *been* up to Balls Pond Road).

'Let's spend all this,' I said.

'Only if you let me spend my ten.'

'Why did *you* bring ten?'

'Well, I thought you might be broke and I had this saved for a hat.'

Greatly moved, I squeezed her knee between mine under the table.

'More hock,' I said.

She picked up the bottle and wagged it. 'Goodness, empty!' she said.

This wasn't the moment for empty bottles, was it?

'Mario!' I screamed.

'*Si, signore.*'

'Two more Schmidt '57. *Lesto lesto.*'

'*Si, signore.*'

'Shall we go to Winston's next?' I said, when the two bottles had been and gone.

'No, darling.'

'But why not?' I said, surprised.

'I don't know.'

It reduced the temperature severely.

'But you can't not like Winston's,' I said, thinking of Bruce and all the lovely lovely people. 'It's simply stuffed with loyals.'

'I'm sorry,' she said. 'I just don't want to go.'

I might have known this would happen. It would mean a dreadful quarrel if I persisted, and that was the last thing I wanted.

I thought for a moment, and then had a bright idea.

'There's only one thing for it, then.'

'What?'

'Paris?'

The old loyal clapped her hands.

'*When?*'

'Now!' I shouted, jumping up and down in my chair.

We rushed about looking for my coat. We paid the jack-and-jill. As it was the Trois Assommeurs, I sorted through my various kiting books and paid with a kosher purple kite which wouldn't bounce. Then we fled into the street and hurled ourselves into the jamjar.

'Oh, what's the time?'

'Only ten-thirty,' I said with glee. 'Plenty of time to catch the midnight plane.'

'How pay our fares? Here's my ten.'

But I thrust it back at her: 'No, no—keep it for river ooze: we'll kite 'em at the airport!'

I switched on the radio and got some top pop on Radio Lux.

'Must go back to Navarre Crescent,' said Christice, 'and pack some things.'

We went back there, and I surveyed the gaff doubtfully.

'Hope the foulsters aren't back,' I said.

'Come in and try if they are,' she whispered, fitting her twirl in the latch. Inside, the hall was empty and silent. Christice looked about for nasty hats and coats, but there weren't any.

'Come on up.'

So we went up, my flesh beginning to creep in that agreeable way it used to in the country when one was very young at house-parties, creeping by moonlight down corridors to a bird's room with one's shoes in one hand and a guilty conscience in the other. In darkness we reached the top of the stairs; by the lamplight from the street we could see the disordered drawing-room as we had left it. There was even a hissing in the corner where we had left the gramophone needle whispering on the final groove of 'South Rampart Street Parade'.

Christice was going upstairs, but I stopped her.

'Here,' I whispered. My scalp prickled as I kissed her there in the silence, the warm summer darkness lapping us round. Then she took her shoes off and stalked softly upstairs in stockinged feet so as not to wake Nanny, who would have wanted us to drink some gin with her in the nursery, but now wasn't the time. So, while she packed up there, I had it away downstairs to a little room with a piano in it, and played a thing I'd invented once at seventeen called Mirage in A Minor. Well, of course I found it difficult, because deviation doesn't leave much time for the piano; but it was based on a tune I learned from my French governess called 'Mon Chat', and I played it only when things were good, very good, like now, or else when I'd made a bomb.

Now there was Christice in the doorway, scuffing the carpet and looking vaguely ready and cramming a spongebag into her coat pocket: and suddenly the splendour of what we were doing caught up with me. It's a sensation which repeats itself each time as if it were new, and I thought how in an hour we were going to be there tearing up the runway with the engines rasping and taking off to turn upwards into the skies.

'The light's on in the drawing-room,' she said.

'Well, I'll go and turn it off.'

'Yes, do. Then we must fly, mustn't we?'

Thinking how lovely and conspiratorial and devious it was, just like Hurlingham, I sped gaily up the flight and flung open the door. There was Lord Chrism standing in the middle of the wrecked drawing-room in his dressing-gown and slippers, smoking a pipe and watching the telly.

'Sorry, wrong door,' I murmured, and took the steps in one leap, but I don't think he saw.

When we got to Paris we made straight for the Left Bank and a darling little joint called L'Escale in Rue Monsieur le Prince, which everyone knows, and we sat up all night at the minute counter, drinking in the chatter of French and Spanish and Arabic and getting the Mexicans to play 'Duque de Lucena' for us, but they didn't know the words so we had to teach it them. And we sat doing a bomb, drinking tequila with a pinch of salt and a suck from a slice of lemon; and that makes the tequila like a gaudy, violent nectar at the back of your throat and your head thuds as if there were a drum in it and it's rather like snap.

'We're in love,' mused Christice sadly, a tear sploshing on the bar—'again.'

Another tequila cheered the old bird up again in no time. But later she approached it another way.

'What are you up to at the moment?' she asked hopelessly. 'I know I mustn't ask, so here I am asking.'

As a matter of fact, this question brought me up with a nasty jolt. It was hours since I'd given a thought to the morries, let alone the project. Then I thought hell, how silly! not being able to tell *her*. For a moment I was tempted to confess all—but only for a moment. For you tell someone . . . so what happens? All you do is clutter them up with something they'd be far better off knowing nothing about; and, besides, it's people's nature to rabbit, especially birds. You can't really blame them for it, even when you find yourself in the nick, and you've got no one to thank for it but yourself. But that doesn't stop the other members of the party arranging for the grass's head to be quietly torn off in a little nook or corner somewhere, does it?

She sensed this, I suppose, because she let it drop; instead she slipped off her stool and we went off to dance. There, on the floor, our original mood slipped away until there was nothing but us cradling each other in our arms and not taking our eyes off each other, and I had to pinch myself and say 'Bulbul' once or twice to make sure it was happening; the huge, carefully educated taboo of sex clambered helplessly up my leg and I felt unarmed—in a mood to swim, to dance, to make love.

We took a train from St. Lazare just as it was getting light and bathed in the river together naked in a bight the Seine makes at Les Andelys; the sky bloomed and the sun rose grandiosely while we were dressing and shivering, and Christice got out her spongebag and made up, using the placid water as a mirror.

We were still drunk when we hitched a ride back to Paris on

the back of a turnip lorry. We held hands and sang most of the way and bought the driver *coups de rouge* at a *tabac* in Pontoise. As I'd knocked for the tickets, we still had half a ton on us and we meant to spend it. But looking at Christice sitting in the drowsy, half-wakened *tabac* I thought strangely: 'The morning for men is peace, but the evening is war'—and don't ask me where it came from, *please*, but it meant or summed up something about Christice and me, and feeling rushed in for a second on a tumult of grief before her laughter shook us and displaced it. Then we were on our way, driving east into the sun, and we laughed and played a game to pass the time called 'Slags and Squares', but I remember feeling glad we never deceived each other.

Walking along the street near the *rondpoint de Saint Germain*, among the soft greys and greens of the trees, it was too hot so we turned off without a word and for the first time since checking in we went up to our room in the Hôtel d'Isly. I drew the curtains and took the phone off the hook.

'What have we come here for?' Christice asked, her face a blur in the red half-dark from the curtains. We made love just as we were, in too much hurry to undress, the things spilling out of the spongebag in Christice's pocket. She made soft noises like an animal, kissing me all over; we made love just as it happened to occur midway on the tide of the day—and in my hands when I held her *there* I felt I held the mystery and key to things which I spent my whole life *not* looking for; so that this natural affair was certainly like an apocalypse and made up for a great many black nights and bulging or boyish shapes, or just old shapes; so that it was like lunch when you're really hungry and just turn in to a restaurant for it, and it was also like a dream you have where everything turns out right and you hold out your hand to the person in the dream, an austere, kind person, like a 1917 parson in norfolk jacket and bicycling clips, and you say: '*Si je meurs puis-je venir avec vous?*' and the voice says '*Volontiers*' and the dream ends.

It was far far better than the love we made when we eloped,

93

and better than after the snap party. I don't know *why* it was better—it was just different somehow.

It was high time to get back to London on the hurry-up. We picked up the motor at London Airport and sped into the city. I let her out in the King's Road and turned to watch her blonde head carry itself casually through the crowd. Then I went straight on to the Tealeaf for a meet with the morries. It wasn't for hours that I suddenly tumbled it was over. But there was no time to think. We had to see Mr. Cream and arrange shooters. Things happen like that. One minute you have them and then the next you haven't. Nothing'll bring them back, or perhaps something will, you never know.

II

FRIDAY was a busy morning. The Archbubble had shelled monkey for exes after a lot of moaning and screaming; this teaming up for the 'off' was like everything else in a morrie's life—it all happened at once. We had to get the tickets, make the reservations, book the car on the ferry, Mike ringing Frankfurt the whole time and fixing the last-minute details of the meet with this Reisemann, big-time legman to the kraut mob.

Don't think we'd gone into all this biz without a lot of thought. Go ask the slag and it'll tell you the morries are nishte when it comes to angst.

But we had it all planned.

When it comes to big-time deviation shooters are a thing you certainly have to consider, for one thing, because, apart from the pain and maybe no-more-gin-and-tonic of it all, it's just bad tactics to go and get yourself drilled.

I put on Marchmare's leopard-skin slippers and padded down to where Mike was waiting to see me in the drawing-room. He was sitting on the best armchair looking sharp enough to cut it. Suddenly he wasn't an out-of-work hood any more. It was, after all, his deal as much as ours and didn't he show it, sitting there like Savile Row divided by two, the cuff-links at four-and-six and the tie-clip all from the one card at Marks and Sparks. When he saw me he uncoiled and came over, hand outstretched. Not thinking, I took it and the next thing I knew I was on my back, hitting the floor with a horrible thump. I looked up with my ears singing in a silence broken only by the sounds of the Archbubble singing and counting his money in the bath.

'Not too clever this morning, are you?' he says. 'You'll have to think a lot quicker than that where you're going. . . . Ah, come on, come over here an' I'll brush you off.'

Which he does.

'O.K. now,' he says, when I'd given us both a vera and settled down, 'I want to have a last run-down with you—I don't suppose I shall see you again before the off.'

'Right,' I said, 'here you are. Marchmare and I take the evening boat to Ostend on Monday afternoon, which arrives at six-forty-five. The Archbubble goes by a different route altogether, taking the air ferry. He arrives with the XK about the same time. You'll leave a day before us and moody about in Amsterdam and then take the train on to Frankfurt from there. Right?'

'Right.'

'Marchmare and I check in at the Frankfurterhof, the Archbubble at the Pariser Hotel. You'll find yourself a nasty grubby little pension somewhere, but make sure there's a private blower. O.K.?'

'O.K.'

'Well, now here's the tricky bit. After Marchmare and I have been at the Frankfurterhof for about an hour, Reisemann will get us on the blower and tell us to take a taxi to the station and then take the third taxi down in the rank outside the main station entrance, inside which I imagine there'll be a hatful of very dodgy figures. You'll ride with the Archbubble in his XK and trail our taxi, and in fact you'll trail us the whole time from that moment on—and you'd better not lose us because you two are all we've got between here and Judgement Day for all I know and I'll tell you straight up and down I don't like it, understand?'

'Nah,' he says, 'there ain't nothing to it.'

'Oh, there ain't nothing to it, isn't there?' says I, stamping my foot. 'Well, it's all very well for you to say that, but to me it looks just like Sherlock bloody Holmes and Professor Moriarty rolled into one with the odds worse than a hundred to eight.'

'Aw,' he says, 'we'll be right behind you.'

'You'd better be,' says I sharply. 'Here we go off to see this load of commies on their own precious manor—one shooter in the loo, another in the wardrobe for all we know, so keep the obbs on us.'

'Now look,' he says, getting the needle, 'I don't want anything to go wrong with this lark any more'n you do.'

'Of course you don't,' says I, 'because if it does none of us'll cop. And that's partly why I want to get all the details straight —and also because there's a hell of a lot of unknowns in it. Going out into the foggy foggy dew to see them on their own manor's potty,' I said. 'It's making us bet up on a deuce in the hole to his pair of aces, or don't you play poker?'

But the point is, the four of us have already had all this out a score of times, but there's just nothing to be done about it, because Reisemann's sitting there holding our loot and the merchandise and he just won't play it any other way. They're the same with deviation as they are with their foreign policy. Take it or leave it. We take it. Still, you can't help feeling alarmed, starting off on someone else's foreign manor way down in the game, and who doesn't know about the krauts like they were in the war, and for all we know thousands of out-of-work S.S. men camping about looking for loonies like us to try out their rusty old Lügers on. I'm not screaming or anything, but that's why I want the whole thing *planned*. There won't be any old Plinth to go running to when we get out there.

'Well,' says Mike, 'and how are you going to play this meet when you get to it?'

'You'll have to leave that to us,' I said rather primly, to disguise the fact that I had no idea. 'But in case anything goes the other way I want to know that you're both out there with the safety-catches off, because if you think the commies treat all this as a joke, I don't.'

'All right, all right,' he says, 'no need to go off alarming about it.'

'No,' I said, 'just as long as we all know where we are.'

'That's all right, morrie,' he says to me, and gives me a winning smile and comes over and slaps me on the back. 'You're my mate,' he says seriously. 'I wouldn't never let anything 'appen to you, boy.'

'Well,' I said, 'we'll have a vera on that, then,' and I pour us out two. And I'm glad of it because I've got the shakes a bit and, as I say, people think that deviation, if it's not just dotty like in the movies, is dead clever and quick like Agatha Christie and Ngaio Marsh wrapped up in one. But it isn't. Come to a rub it's a few precautions, careful planning, being more-handed than the others and then, in the death, just a bet like you shoot at crap, straight win or lose. And while the whole deal may be straight up and down, then again it may not, and I'm not taking a single chance with commies, not one.

And that's not all. I've had the feeling Old Bill's had the obbs on us very closely, ever since that night at Winston's, when Plinth saw Mike and me in there together.

You just can't play it too cool.

'Transporting the slush,' Mike was saying, 'you'll do in the spare tyre of your motor. Cream'll fix all that for you. And you'd better carry your shooters that way as well.' He scribbled on a piece of paper. 'Leave the jam outside the Tealeaf and Cream's boys'll take it away. Then you can pick it up again later from where it says here.' He gave me the paper swallowing his vera, and took himself off.

I went downstairs to dress, thinking God here I go through Dover Customs and here I come back with a cool quarter of a million in dud beehives: I-drove-for-the-Führer morrie at the wheel, camping about in front of the Customs boys trying to look like a second lieutenant in the Ordnance Corps coming back to barracks after a dirty weekend on the continong. To the *North* . . . all this to the North to the *North*'s a shame, really, because it's a waste; we got to the North long ago, stopped for a quick vera and then said to the *North* again because we never dreamed this dreary old place could be IT, the North—with no trad jazz and bird, after all. Looking back, you can see how that quick touch in the Ritz bar or that vin-blanc-cassis outside the French frontier café at Béhobie after the tape-recorders must have been the North, and you can see how krautland too is probably going to be *it*, the precarious North, with Marchmare, the Archbubble and me holding the bridge, after which homespun cobblers I shall have it away in the jam and see you in the Tealeaf.

12

I T WAS a morning of brisk trade in the Tealeaf, down to its being Saturday, no doubt. The boozer's in a select little street off Park Lane surrounded by little peewee pink-and-white houses where the arch grafters on a paper income of twenty grand a year live it up on an actual minus five; and clapped-out Bentleys dream away their H.P. contracts on a tea-cupful of gas like Chelsea pensioners on wheels, while upstairs punters for moody poker are chatted up with plenty of vera lynn.

The saloon bar of the Tealeaf's reserved mostly for squares and grasses, and a hatful of kosher figures—also writ-servers who congregate thither, knowing it's a morrie's hideaway, so you have to be all about trout and be careful not to get one slapped on you as you go in.

Through the back, though—in a bar which might once have been painted a moody delinquent pink—a lot of rather nasty lunch is spooned down by a mort of capifigs. Only such law as revels in the rank of chief inspector and above is filtered past the boiled orb of Joe Llewellyn, the Welsh who rules the joint, and these are old hands who know better than to transgress the rules, and sit in a corner of the bar keeping themselves to themselves, content with a telly aerial hidden inside their hats and keeping careful obbs on the new arrivals.

Pushing our way through now against the *va-et-vient*, March-mare and I gain this haven, to be rewarded at once by the sight of Messrs. Copewood and Cream, purveyors of shooters, etc., to the trade, who, with their followers, queen it from a table near the bar, where they feed steak to a snarling hound and rack their ganglia over the race-page of the linens. A quick butchers shows up Old Bill three-handed, also a particularly nasty female grass—and if looks were acid baths the two she collects from us would reduce her to gristle quicker than Mrs. Durand-Deacon. Three aged punters, one with a gumboil, a bookie, a card-grafter and a *chargé* from one of those new spade republics noshing in a corner complete the tale. Something too vague to be called a look passes between us and Mr. Cream, so we turn to the bar and order a vera. Marchmare opens a linen and I, naturally, try to clock the mutterings of Old Bill on my left, but of course it's no go, so I give up and steer over to the broads operator—the same as saw me all right that night at Mrs. Byrd's game. Now two boilers appear with their mugs, their years tied up in their headscarves, and at that moment Mr. Cream elects to scarper to the blower outside on the stairs, moving slowly from his table feeling in his pockets for change. The law get up, swallowing their feeble beer, and leave, and I see them right out of the door—and that minute Mr. Cream replaces the blower and vanishes into the ladies loo where merchandise and loot, coy of the public gaze, are habitually exchanged and cut up—in fact, as soon as the law's gone it's back to normal in the Tealeaf and biz as usual. Mr. Copewood, the heavy, splits a match cleanly down the middle with his front teeth and beckons to Marchmare. When he's gone over I moisher off and join Mr. Cream in the ladies, and pick up my raincoat as I go by.

Mr. Cream, a right heavy, sits carelessly on the loo. He is dark and broody-looking; his movements are slow, quick-quick-slow, as he crosses one nicely polished brogue over his knee and you see the steel tip—one of the most fearsome hoods in the biz . . . not to say Mister to him would be asking for a wack from Mr. Copewood, or they might put the boot in and probably break your leg, so it's safer not to hand out any aggravation.

Especially when he talks, Mr. Cream looks gloomy and heartbroken behind his twenty-guinea binns, like a Battersea Park front window-pane in a drizzle. So there's several reasons why he's known in the trade as 'Funeral' Cream. He gazes at me now, sad as December.

'Lock it,' he says, meaning the door. I do. Outside I just have a peep at his two heavies taking up inconspicuous positions. No old boiler's going to wag her puff in here for a bit.

'Right,' says Mr. Cream, jerking his head, 'three shooters. Let's 'ave the loot.'

So I out ninety in beehives and Mr. Cream counts it with a huge forefinger and stows it in his hunting waistcoat. Then he picks up an attaché case from the floor beside him and snaps it open. From it he takes three packages done up in oily rags.

'They're all different, see?' says Mr. Cream, in a tone of deep despair. 'I couldn't help that. But they're all good an' they're not hot. One .38 Colt revolver. Nice old shooter—clumsy but lots of stopping power. One .32 Walther and a 9 mm. Parabellum for neat work.'

'Yes,' I said, 'that'll be mine, Mr. Cream.'

'Ever used a shooter?' inquires Mr. Cream, in a voice near to tears.

Well, I so nearly had in Spain that I put in a lot of practice out at a *placita* in a suburb of Madrid.

'Colt throws up a bit when she fires,' intoned Mr. Cream desperately. 'So don't any of you use her over ten yards or someone'll 'ave your guts for a garter.' He picks up the two autos first, double-shuffling the actions and snapping them at a fly squashed on the mirror over the basin.

Outside I hear a roar of laughter at some joke. I stuff the Parabellum in my pants pocket and the Walther in the raincoat.

'That's it,' says Mr. Cream paternally, 'that's it, you've got it.'

Then he slips open the Colt and spins the chamber idly in his fingers as if reluctant to part. 'That's the 'eavy one, as I was saying,' says Mr. Cream dispassionately. 'Do well to cover a party from behind a door or suchlike. The 'eavy one,' he repeats fondly, handing it to me, 'and 'ere's the ammo for it. Hundred rounds. Now,' he says, wagging his finger at me, 'you put all that gear in the motor this afternoon—the boys'll show you where, when you go down to pick 'er up. And here,' he said, handing over two more oily boxes, 'is the ammo for the others . . . it's clearly marked,' he added, 'which is which, so don't get it mixed now,' and he tried to smile, but it was such agony that it nearly cracked his boat-race and he had to give it up.

'Well,' said Mr. Cream with a yawn, getting up from his perch with unconscious dignity, 'that's it, then. Don't know why I do these things for no-good little ponces like you . . . still, give the younger generation a chance, I says . . . oh, and just one thing—you've paid the hire on them for thirty days, no more, and so if I don't get them back you'd better watch out. Count fifty slow before yer come out,' says Mr. Cream, going straight to the door and out of it—and that was that, as the nursery rhyme puts it.

Next Marchmare and I went down to collect the motor; we took a taxi to Fulham Broadway Underground and then started to walk. Marchmare had the Walther on him and the Colt and the Parabellum were now in my raincoat, banging uncomfortably against my hips. We dug our chins into our necks because it was pouring with rain; I looked up just once and saw the grey clouds scudding above, nearly grazing the drab buildings and thought: 'Christ, I'm not very fit: long time since I did much of this shank's lark, too much boozing away in bars.' I looked sideways at Marchmare; he was springing agilely along without a care in the world, humming 'The Texas Ranger', which I knew he was inwardly attaching to the unspeakable words of 'Texas Alexis', which he used to sing in Torremolinos nightclubs.

Presently we reached a dead-end alley on our right; there was a bomb-site on the corner of it with a handful of motors, a '53 Vauxhall marked 'Sound Runner' and a '48 Mark V, which was easy work for the boost-up boys, settling grimly into the cinders on flat tyres. Above them flapped a wet, yellow banner which read: 'We Have A Buyer For Your Second Hand Car.' At the blocked end of the alley loomed a petrol pump with the paint scaling from it, and a glass door on its right bore the word 'Office' and above it the suggestive name of 'Noakes'. It wasn't at all kosher.

'Well, here we are,' I said brightly, walking in. Inside, a gipsy in a mauve suit was sitting at a table reading a horror comic. He didn't look up when we came in, a trick he must have been practising for years.

We closed the door and leaned against it. I dropped my raincoat on a chair. The atmosphere was rather tense.

'Nice little joint they've got here,' said Marchmare at last to no one special, 'and such *kosher* manners.'

'Yes,' I said, 'fancy the creep wanting to put us in a bad temper. He must be potty, mustn't he?'

The gipsy looked up a bit sharply at that. 'Ever been bottled and razored?' he said.

It was all over in three seconds. Marchmare moved like light. The table went over with a hollow bang and there was a thick smack as the edge of his hand cracked on to the bridge of the gipsy's nose. That entertaining person wound up with his head against the wall.

'No,' said Marchmare, 'and you aren't going to break my duck, darling.'

There was a lot of blood about. I was glad it had happened.

'Now,' I said, helping myself to his snout and flicking the match at him, 'you'd better ask who sent us, hadn't you? And mind your manners.'

No answer.

'You heard, crumb,' said Marchmare.

'Heard what?' said a voice behind us.

We stood still.

'Well, who did send you, then?' pursued the voice.

'It was Funeral,' we said, without turning round.

'That's O.K., then, isn't it?' said the voice, 'We can all relax. I'm Noakes.'

So we turned round then and there was a ponce, natty as a TV producer, waving a swagger-stick. 'Come on through the back,' he invited, in his rollicking kosher tones, flicking the stick. He was a sort of grammar-school morrie, though, really, and wore cheap soiled suèdes. 'By the way,' he said, humming and tutting at us as we followed him down some concrete steps underground, 'you ought to remember infantry tactics and keep one leg on the ground. Bren section cover the advance at right angles. That's what they taught me at Sandhurst, anyway. Both of you doing the poor little bleeder at once like that. I'm surprised at you,' he said, tittupping down the concrete steps.

There wasn't anything to be said to this, so we very properly stayed stumm and said nothing. That little fight had done me good; I felt calmer now and booked into the adventure; I hadn't had a really decent fight since the night of my birthday in a little caff off the Gloucester Road.

We came into a big hangar littered with jamjars, and there was ours out in the middle, gleaming and powerful, with the seats stripped out of it and the spare tyre out and off its wheel. Three men were working on it with thin cotton gloves so as not to leave dabs. One wore a fatigue cap and was a negro: I guessed an American deserter.

'Ah, they're not quite ready yet,' said the ponce.

'It's all right,' said Marchmare. 'Plenty of time.'

One of the boys, a blond with his nose bashed flat to his cheeks and a nasty scar on his chin which seemed to have been done with a mailbag needle, came up to the ponce with his hands held up and fluttering in the weirdest way I've seen.

The ponce turned to me. 'Let's have those shooters and the ammo,' he said. 'Time for them to go in the nest now. Such *lovely* toys,' he said, regretfully handing them over to the fluttery ice-cream, who took them over to the motor, balancing them in his hands.

'Willy's a dummy,' added the ponce, 'lucky for you it wasn't him you mixed it with up there. He'd've topped you for sure.'

'Dummies don't squeal,' said Marchmare, thinking aloud.

'Oo, you *doo* catch on quick!' said the ponce in that nasty way.

'Yes,' I said, getting the dead needle, 'even if we did never make it to Sandhurst.'

'Watch it now, masochist,' said the ponce, licking his lips.

We watched him very closely, and, boy, if it had gone the other way we'd never have had a chance, not there on the away ground. But he must have thought about Mr. Cream, because after a second he shrugged and just smacked that little stick of his against his leg—but I realized it was only fear of Mr. Cream that stopped him putting the boys on to us so they could hold us while he cut us to bits with it. Charming. It was suddenly all too plain why he hadn't gone down at Sandhurst and afterwards in the 4th Gorgons or whatever. Well, well, I thought, philosophically, it just shows how everyone finds their little niche in life. And I walked over to the motor to see what they were doing to it.

It was really very crafty. They had taken the steel plate right out which supports the back seat, and to the underside of this they were screwing three oblong boxes in a row, which held the shooters and the shells for them. The boxes were so placed that they could not be seen even when the motor was examined from underneath, for they lay in a line along the top of the prop-shaft housing. Best of all, it was dead simple and if there was a short delay getting the shooters out of the motor across the Channel, well, wasn't that a terrible thing!

A quarter of a million quid in beehives in bundles of five hundred pounds makes five hundred bundles—and the ponce had had the tyre taken off the wheel and, by using old linens for notes, showed us how the bundles would fit. It was a squeeze —it's amazing, when you stop to think of it, how much space that number of beehives really takes up, even when the notes are brand new. The ponce had the boys show us how to get it back on the wheel with a couple of tyre-levers without damaging the merchandise. Once it was back it looked like a perfectly normal tubeless tyre blown up rather hard. And nothing more, even under the closest inspection. We'd arrange it so that our return would be on the busiest boat of the day, with all the ice-creams coming back from their little potter to Cannes, or wherever the squares go, so that the Customs boys wouldn't find time to give the jam anything like a proper going-over, unless it were down to right sus.

I looked at the ponce to congratulate him on this neat bit of edgar wallace, but he didn't seem to expect it so I stayed stumm. It was really weird, though, to watch these bastards who'd have shivved us for a Bovril tidily packing shooters and ammo away for us as calm as butlers getting a picnic ready for a summer's day. They hopped under the motor for a minute, checking finally, tightening screws and making certain nothing showed. Then they slid from under, banged the boot shut and we were home and dry—and from here on we'd be driving a very very hot jamjar—short of a downright murdermobile, the hottest, maybe.

Following the ponce up the stairs while his bent boys drove the motor on to the ramp and into the upper air, I began to feel a bit dazed and have a dry mouth and wish I had my crystal ball so's I could see what was going to happen.

It was a good thing I couldn't.

'I'll tell you what, morrie,' I said, as Marchmare and I drove off back up the King's Road, 'I think it'd be a good idea if you and I spent the weekend at Tumbledown before taking off. Otherwise we've got the whole of this evening and Sunday to get through with nothing to do but twiddle our thumbs.'

'Where is Tumbledown?' he said languidly, stretching himself in the seat and throwing a fireball at a passing bird.

'Right on the A20, fifty miles from Dover.'

'What's the *idea*, though, morrie? I do hate parents so.'

'Well, I'll tell you what it is,' I said. 'I'd like to have a go at practising with those shooters. And the stableyard at Tumble-down's simply perfect—there's no other house round it for miles.'

Marchmare's face at once lit up. 'Ah,' he said with gleaming minces. 'Shooter-practice! Yes, now that's a *good* idea.'

'All right,' I said, aiming the jar at Rome Street and sending a milk-float driver into a fit, 'let's pick up our gear and go.'

13

As we arrived at Tumbledown the sun came out. We turned into the drive, and after a moment of drifting under poplars in full leaf we came to the house. I drew into that corner of the sweep particularly reserved for *visitors*, and stopped well away from my pa's old Bentley, which after a lot of haggling and going ahead the old darling had paid too much for and wasn't nearly as good as the jar I could have got him along Warren Street for half the loot.

Of course, its name isn't Tumbledown, but the word describes the house so perfectly that I've let it stand without thought of alteration since I first clocked the gaff in my grandparents' time at the age of nine. It rears up like the latest monster on the movie hoardings in Piccy Circus, its façade frowning furiously into the sunset. It's not the sort of place I should care to put a date to. The front door and the *hall* are Tudor; but wanting to go modern in 1860 my great-grandmother (an angry old boiler with a stick who married a lord *en secondes noces* when she was seventy and did good works sending socks to the Empress of Austria's shipwreck funds) got busy with the firm who was hard at work on her jerry-building schemes in South Ken. What Tumbledown ended up as isn't easy to explain; the old odd-ball built two-thirds of a new house—or, rather, a threatening diatribe in red-and-mauve brick, which, reaching its peroration somewhere in the gables, winds up in a roaring skyline of thirty spiky chimneys grinding their teeth in an astonished sky between the rigidly extended fascist arms of two brand-new and very mixed-up towers—the whole roof fairly buzzing on a windy day with dozens of little weather-vanes. It gives you rather a headache if you look at it too long: it's wearying, like Caliban buttonholing you in hell and telling you the struggle he's having trying to get along with himself. Even the two presentable towers, perched high up the garden by some Tudor ice-cream, are ruined—by my parents this time, who condescend to people over them with such horrid awe that they, too, departed early from my dream world. And the last pair fell to Great-Grandma's turn again; this time she incorporated the hapless things into the stables, a really *big* blot which she cemented and then stuccoed on to the countryside shortly after her return from a trip to Germany where she had been much impressed, I was told, by Neuwannstein. But I privately think our Ludwig would have been a bit envious of Tumbledown.

'*God!*' said Marchmare, getting out of the motor, in that per-jorative tone not unmixed with awe to which I was no stranger.

In the many shadows three people were very busy not doing things. The chauffeur was wringing out a cloth behind Pa's car, the gardener was not mowing the lawn he had started on when he gave notice, and my great-aunt, who had flown down for the weekend, darling, in 1929, during which the slump neatly swallowed every penny she had, was sitting in the rose-garden reading the same paperback she had begun on my return from America a year ago.

No one seemed to have registered our arrival properly, so I slammed the car door. Everyone jumped and looked guilty. They were none of them too keen on me, because I had made it perfectly clear that when my turn came at Tumbledown, if it ever did, I should institute a very different regime, inaugurating it by giving the lot of them their cards.

'Well, mowing as ever?' I said to the gardener, and to the chauffeur chattily: 'Nice day for mopping about with cars, Toade, eh?'

Feeling it was my round, I was now ready for the mute Polish servant who came creeping along the *pavé*, in response to my sonata on the doorbell, to take our things. That's to say, he was mute in our presence, but made up for it amply by hurling insults at the polyglot cook in the kitchen.

'Well, Jablonski?' I said sharply. 'Nice evening.'

He murmured something politely, doubtless remembering, as I certainly was, the dramatic incidents which had led up to my mother confiscating his whips—also the hold I had had on him ever since the night I met him in the village pub, where, in a moment of over-confidence, he had whipped out for my inspection a snapshot of himself dressed as a *feldwebel* standing in front of a long line of featureless huts and a smoking chimney.

'How's the photograph collection? And the whips?' said I cheerily.

He eyed me dumbly. A far cry from Jeeves.

'Goodness,' said Marchmare, who was staring around him. 'I can just see us saying: "Hola, varlet, a stoup of wassail there! Ho, there, Gapgrin, where she comes!"'

'Yes,' I said.

As a matter of fact, I was not looking forward any too much to my reunion with my mother: I owed her about three ton, and a lot more on the old in her little black book.

We went through the hall. There was no one about—except of course the pictures, particularly the Jordaens with its sinister drunken figures *au premier plan*. A shotgun bellowed on the lawn, and the remains of smoke and music airily looped the chandelier from the glass roof above us. Beneath the gallery, which led out of sight under arches of stained deal, a piano stood open. I glanced at the music lying suggestively on top of it. It was a collection of Vivaldi *concerti*, not scored for the piano anyway, which belonged to me—one of my father's little attempts at an atmosphere of culture which as usual had gone lightly wrong. As I had feared, Marchmare, peering over my shoulder, commented on it.

III

'Nice piano,' he said maliciously.

'Unfortunately,' I replied sombrely, 'no one can really play it.'

The house was dizzily still, except for the light tittering of my mother's voice upstairs as she spoke to the cook about dinner down the vulcanite house-tube. The deceptiveness of the peaceable atmosphere was showing already—the spectres of old rows, screams, punishment and unintelligibly opposite views were sharply present, and as usual I was beginning to wish I hadn't come.

My father appeared in the drawing-room doorway, his demob hat on his head and a gun under his arm. A dead pigeon dangled from his left hand, which was swathed in a mitten. He surveyed us for a moment in silence. He looked very severe, but he was really rather frightened, whether by Marchmare or myself or both it was still too early to say. The defence mechanisms he employed were, I noted, greatly over-compensated as usual; the battling brows, the mouth drawn tight and grim under the sparse Lancers moustache, were amply betrayed by the light, lifelike shivering of the pigeon's body.

'Just missed yer tea,' he growled, ignoring the introductions. 'Yer mother's upstairs. Be back in a minute—just gotter deposit my pigeon. Wait in the drawing-room.' And he was gone.

I looked carefully at Marchmare to see how he was taking all this, but he looked impassively straight ahead. However, I was sure he would laugh afterwards, and after all, I thought, for God's sake why not? It was time I got Tumbledown out of my system for good and exorcized it. Meanwhile, at least our motor with its shooters and peculiar spare wheel had receded into phantasy for the time being. I was not sorry.

I wasn't quick enough getting Marchmare into the drawing-room. My mother caught us, as if in the act of *doing* something, arresting us with a look halfway downstairs. She was wearing a new silk dress and was evidently going out. She carried a cart-wheel hat and elbow-length black gloves.

Guiltily, I presented Marchmare, who looked quite impossible, though it was hard to decide just how. He stood loungingly near me, shifting his weight from one foot to the other, and I felt that if I didn't look out he might start things off badly by doing something diabolical, though I couldn't decide quite what.

It looked like the beginning of a sticky couple of days.

'What are you going to *do* here?' asked my mother sharply.

'Do?' I said vaguely. It was difficult to tell her, in a watered-down but convincing way, exactly what we were going to *do*.

'Yes,' said my mother, '*do*. I'm not really a bit pleased to see either of you, and if I see so much as the hat of a newspaper reporter or a policeman while you're here out you both go directly.'

Marchmare made an incomprehensible noise.

My mother looked at him exceedingly sharply. 'And I might add,' she said, 'that I'm not going to have the house turned into a bear garden. You can put that idea right out of your heads, the pair of you.' Her glance embraced us equally in castigation.

'Oh, there won't be anything like that, you know,' I said.

We all walked into the drawing-room and arranged ourselves round the tea-table, and my mother rang for clean cups. I had never seen the old bird haughtier and crosser.

'And how long are the pair of you proposing to stay?' she inquired grimly.

'Oh, only a couple of days,' I said.

'We're going over to Germany on Monday,' remarked Marchmare casually.

'What for? Pleasure, I suppose.'

'No, no, on business sort of,' he said, waving his hand.

I could have told him that this sort of approach with my mother would never do; the vaguer you were, the sharper she became. It would never do to have her pressing for details; we had no story ready. But it was too late.

My mother shot me her sharpest look so far. 'But I thought you were supposed to be broke,' she said.

Marchmare snuffled irritatingly into his tea. It was not lost on the inquisitor. I shuffled my feet. I had had no idea it was going to be as bad as this. 'Well, I was, you know,' I said, 'but I picked up a bit racing the other day.'

My mother looked heavenwards, and I realized I had made another blunder. 'Disgusting,' she said and I hoped she'd scarper off on that tack for a bit. But glancing up from my plate I found myself hypnotized by those twin barrels again.

'Well, in that case,' she remarked, 'if you have a little money you and I had better take ourselves off for a short talk—if,' she added with poisonous sweetness, 'your young friend will allow it.'

I shuddered under these shrewd blows, and was in the act of catching Marchmare's attention to get him to create a diversion of *any* kind when, thank goodness, my father came in at last carrying his mittens, without which he found it difficult to shoot nowadays or, it might equally be, in lonely imitation of the aged and crotchety duke he had shot with last winter while I was in the States.

'Dammit,' he said to me, wandering up and down the drum like some lost soul from an officers' mess, 'yer might have warned in.' He too was cross. His routine had been upset; he'd already had his tea and it would have been 'bad form' to 'warn in' again. Now his wife was involved with these two infernal young people and he had no one to talk to except himself.

My mother forced herself to be more agreeable. 'Your father and I are going out this evening,' she remarked, pouring herself some more tea.

'Oh, really?' I said, feeling like Malcolm inquiring after his father's murderer, 'to whom?'

'To the Gooches'.'

I could not suppress a low whistle. Marchmare looked up like a terrier. 'Low-life punters,' I got across to him on the quick wire while my mother was reaching for scones. Whereupon he sat back and left the initiative to me.

'Sounds rather fun,' I said carelessly.

'Meaning you want to come,' said my mother with a cunning

look, which was no doubt meant to make us think she was being no end kosher and dodgy.

'I wouldn't mind,' I said humbly, 'if you wouldn't.'

'And your young friend?'

I wished silently that she wouldn't refer to Marchmare in this way, who, if he had ever been young, was certainly looking old today.

'I should love it,' he said, polite as a sentence out of a French exercise and squinting at his cuff-links in the fading sunlight.

'Damned if I wanter go out,' groaned my father from the other end of the room, where he had now settled in his armchair like the captain of the battleship *Potemkin*. I rather warmed to the old pet. Fearfully mean though he was when it came to finance, he was a lonely and ageing soul. Nothing was all he knew and all he had ever needed to know. Besieged by the Press that time in '56, when they wanted to know if it was true I was running a chain of brothels in Lancaster Gate, they told me how he had clutched his gun more firmly, stared at a point above the reporter's head, and said *he* didn't know but he wouldn't be a bit surprised, bringing my mother down on him like a ton of bricks and earning himself several thousand quid in libel suits if he'd only known. All he wanted now was my mother to say: 'Oh, come on, Edward, you know you're simply aching to go,' and he would have leaped for the stairs like one of his own stags to change into his 1932 flannels and B.B. tie.

What my mother in fact said was: 'I quite agree with you, Edward. You know you simply hate the Gooches.'

No one could blame him for that. They were frightful. But they were also very rich, so I had avoided an open break; they lived at a truly terrible house with a swimming-pool which smelled of chlorine and weeds, and they had two Rollses, one of which was for the *boys*—and that really is rather terrible, isn't it? Only Elinor Glyn could have got away with that sort of thing, and the Gooches didn't attempt to be anything like her. I had been dying to give them a good soaking for years, and with

Marchmare in the district (provided no one recognized him) this might not be impossible. I decided to tackle him about it when we went up to change.

And so, mercifully, tea ended. But the next move, which was to walk round in a ring like those poor people in *The Waste Land*, was hardly more promising.

'Well?' said my mother, 'what do you young things want to do now?'

She knew perfectly well that I could have dyed her orange for saying that. What I wanted was a drink, or a diversion, or both. I felt I was sitting on a keg of gunpowder. Any minute Marchmare might decide to start something, and anything could happen then.

Sure enough, before I could raise a finger the worst occurred.

Marchmare leaned across to my father.

'Excuse me, sir?'

These were the first words they had exchanged directly.

'Well?' said the old darling. 'Well, well? Eh?'

'Couldn't help noticing several very fine pictures in the hall, sir,' said Marchmare deferentially.

'Couple of good primitives, a pair of de Loutherbergs, a Jordaens,' grunted the old thing. 'Well? Know something about pictures? Eh?'

I crossed my fingers and began to pray: who was to tell the old dear that Marchmare and art were not—well, exactly strangers to each other?

'The light's very poor for looking at pictures,' I said angrily.

But my father was already on his feet and halfway to the hall —if there was one thing he liked better than shooting and play-ing jolly songs on the piano it was showing his pictures to visitors: it didn't matter if they were deaf-mutes, as it was a monologue. As he was very mean, though, he had few oppor-tunities for this—and I will say this for him, he always said exactly the same things about all of them.

I watched the withdrawal of my support with dull apprehension.

'I don't like that young man,' said my mother, directly Marchmare was out of the room.

'But you've barely met him.'

'I don't *care*. I've already decided he's a *rotten* influence.'

'What?' I said feebly. 'On me?'

My mother gave a sharp laugh.

'Oh, well,' I said, 'he's not such a bad old bird.'

But she had lost interest in the subject of Marchmare. 'About money . . .' she began.

'Yes, well, now look here it's no use our talking about that,' I said on a rising inflection, like a startled duck getting off the home pond on a frosty morning. 'Darling,' I said, thinking hard and using a tone of exaggerated affection which sometimes worked, 'I've put you at the very top of my short list.' Before she could say anything I lowered my voice and added: 'Matter of fact, talking of money, I was only thinking of something coming down in the car. Now look. This German business is something very special and the thing is I haven't got a nice pair of cuff-links. Not what you'd call a *nice* pair. Now I've rather had my eye on a pair like Marchmare's and I——'

'No,' said my mother angrily.

You'd have thought my experience with Mrs. Marengo would have counted for something, wouldn't you? Still, it had headed her off other more disagreeable subjects. I squeezed her arm, and I must admit: she sort of smiled.

At this moment there were sounds of raucous laughter and bonhomie in the hall. I could hardly believe they were Marchmare's and my father's, but a moment later in they burst, the old darling choking and cracking his fingers and going ahead as if it were 1915 all over again, and Marchmare just telling him the end of a risqué joke I knew all too well, which he kept specially for the older generation. It was about the Duquesa de Riofrio, whom he had done something dreadful with in the ladies side of the Sport Club Real in Madrid.

Marchmare had done it again.

'Well, you people?' said the old pet, beaming at us all. 'A drink?'

My mother looked at him coldly, as if he were crazed.

But in half a minute the corks were popping; in fact, Marchmare had quite a struggle with the vermouth, which hadn't been opened for months. Five minutes later the gin bottle was empty, for Marchmare was showing the old thing how he made one of his special martinis, my father cracking his fingers for joy and peering excitedly over his shoulder.

My mother and I finally prised them apart and I took Marchmare up 'to slip', as he put it to my father, 'into something loose'. On my own responsibility I allotted him a bedroom in quick reversal of what I knew my mother had in store for him (the schoolroom, which was haunted by a growling and bearded nanny). My choice was the North Room: a place with a certain pathos and even grandeur, of such frightening ugliness, due to my great-grandmother, that it had acquired a cavernous tortured beauty of its own, like a Spanish martyr.

Marchmare dumped his pigskin case (which I knew he had stolen from the Archbubble) on to the bed and unzipped it.

'What do you think of the room?' I said.

'Very restful,' he said, his voice rolling hollowly back at him from the marble cornices. 'I think the after-six,' he murmured, 'for the Gooches,' pulling out a white tuxedo which I *saw* him steal practically off an American's back after a night of dodgy poker in Cagnes-sur-Mer. 'One can always pretend to be going on somewhere. . . . Now,' he said briskly, plugging in his Remington razor under the shocked gaze of 'La Bacchante', 'what's the strength with these Gooch people?'

I filled in the details for him.

'What do you think?' he said. 'Poker? Baccarat?'

'Baccarat?' I said, staggered. 'Where?'

'Here, silly.'

'Are you *mad*?'

'Fancy your not knowing how to handle your own

father,' said Marchmare reproachfully, using a Landseer as a mirror.

'Well,' I said defensively, 'you can't handle your ma.'

'Yellow streak down your back, morrie!'

'Anyway, where's the kit?'

'In the motor, of course,' he said impatiently. 'Under the seat. Next to the marked broads. I thought we could leave it here and collect it on our way back.'

'The Gooches would never wear it.'

'Perhaps they wouldn't. What're their drinks like?'

'Oh, they'll be all right,' I said confidently. 'They haven't been rich long enough to learn to be mean about them yet.'

There was a pause while he struggled into a silk Charvet shirt that had never been made for him but fitted him exactly (extraordinary about Marchmare how he seemed to shrink or expand in sympathy with other people's clothes).

'On the whole, I think dodgy poker at their gaff would probably be easier.'

'So do I.'

'I just thought your father might *enjoy* a game of baccarat. He's quite loyal, isn't he?'

'Better than the old battle-axe, anyway.'

He pointed to his coat pocket while he tied his tie. 'Flask in there. Some of your father's V.S.O.P. Have some.'

'I—I didn't know he had any.'

'Whipped it while the old ice-cream was going off about some picture or other. Hope he doesn't lamp my dabs in the dust on the bottle.'

I poured some into a tooth-tumbler and was about to hand it to him, then changed my mind and downed it all myself. Boy, I needed it.

It was eleven o'clock on Sunday morning.

'Here we are,' I said, leading the way into the stableyard.

Marchmare looked about him thoughtfully.

'I wonder how easy it'd be defending a place like this?' he

murmured, eyeing the cement battlements and the crumbling cruciform windows in the coachman's old gaff, which I suppose Victorians fondly imagined were the sort of thing Normans used to fire arrows through.

'I don't quite get you,' I said.

'Oh, you never know,' said Marchmare, 'in case the peasants suddenly decided to rise or something.'

'Oh, I see,' I answered, reflecting that Tumbledown had got him in its toils after all, and trying to picture the village grocer at the head of an angry mob, waving a fistful of unpaid jack-and-jills.

'Well,' said Marchmare briskly, 'to business, morrie.'

We got out the shooters. My parents, mercifully, had gone to church and were out to lunch. We had Tumbledown to ourselves for the afternoon. It seemed to quake at the prospect, shimmering in the hot sun. Birds tittered and croaked in the ilex tree above us; a bumble-bee ambled past. Marchmare drew a bead on it with the Walther and fired. He missed the bee and the bullet smacked on the parapet of the girdling wall and knocked a three-inch chip off it.

'Nice shooter,' he said appreciatively.

'Poor shooting though,' I said, working a shell into the breach of the Parabellum.

He looked at me crossly. He looked simply frightful, as if he had spent the night on Victoria Station with a pint of meths. But then he had been working very hard at the Gooches—we took a hundred and forty quid off those nasty boys of theirs while the grown-ups were still quacking over the second jug of martini. It had had its exciting and difficult moments, as when Marchmare accidentally dealt one of the Gooches a hand that was intended for me. An American girl, too, had joined in. She turned out to be an excessively good player, which threatened to upset the party. But Marchmare luckily recovered his form and dealt seconds off the pack and aces back to back with the dexterity of a veteran off the Mississippi paddleboats. '*Such* a nasty girl, that Josie,' he said to me, as we cut up the cash proceeds in quiet triumph on the Gooches' sundial, 'I was determined she shouldn't spoil things.'

Later in the evening, after the third V.S.O.P., when we were all gathered round the piano, I learned that Marchmare had discounted the Gooch kite with my father for cash—an unheard of event that left my mother and I goggling at each other.

'I like the feller,' I heard him say to her above the chords of the Eton Boating Song.

'Nonsense, Edward. He's dreadful, quite *dreadful*.'

'Such a fine, upstanding little *royalist*,' remarked my great-aunt firmly, speaking for the first time since we had arrived.

'You oughter hear his stories about that Riofrio girl of his,' cackled the old dear. 'Nice bit o' Spanish stuff for a sweet tooth.'

It would have been a shame to tell him that the duchess had begun life as the daughter of a stationmaster in the Midlands.

'I don't suppose she even exists,' said my mother defiantly. 'And I don't for one moment believe she's a real duchess,' she added, skimming uncomfortably close to the truth.

'Haven't heard a feller tell better stories since Fatty Buttulph left the regiment in 'twenty-one,' said my father, plunging into 'Chanson de Florian'.

'Fabulous,' I said to Marchmare afterwards, as we went up to bed. 'Whatever did you *do*?'

'Oh, just flannelled the old ice-cream a bit.'

'I believe you slipped him a love potion or something,' I said severely.

The two of them were inseparable. My mother had had a hellish time dragging him off to church this morning.

'What we want now,' said Marchmare, returning briskly to the present, 'is lots of old bottles.'

There were plenty in the dustbin. While we were foraging in it Toade strolled past, smoking his Sunday pipe. Unfortunately, he saw the butt of Marchmare's shooter poking out of his pocket.

'What's that you've got there?' snarled the socialist Toade.

'It's a nasty horrid shooter,' said Marchmare calmly, taking it out and caressing it fondly.

'Bet yer 'aven't a licence for it,' said Toade, recoiling a pace.

'And I shall aim it at you and pull the trigger,' said Marchmare, 'if you don't go away, you nasty man.'

'I've a good mind to have the law on you,' said Toade, almost out of sight.

'You do that, you horrid old grass,' said Marchmare.

We filled our arms with bottles and walked off. Back in the yard we set up the bottles in a row. I took the first. I was a bit high, but the bottle disappeared in a cloud of powdered glass and the ricochet whined off into the garden.

'Strong medicine,' said Marchmare seriously, demolishing the second bottle. 'Increase the range.'

We stepped back to fifteen yards. Soon all the bottles had gone. Marchmare looked at his watch. It was nearly twelve.

'Time for our little game,' he remarked.

I glanced at the wall, disfigured by an ugly lateral scar as though a firing-squad had been there.

'All right,' I said.

We split up. I won the toss and elected to hide, so I scrambled as silently as I could into the loft above the harness-room, which had once been used as a store for fodder. Instead of windows there was a double door in the wall fifty feet from the ground. I opened the top half a crack; looking down I could see Marchmare in the yard below, his face to the wall, counting up to ninety. When he had finished he shouted 'Coming' and slipped off through the door which led back up the steps we had taken coming from the garden. At once I knew what he would do. He would go through the rose-garden, round the back of the house and approach the yard from the back drive. There was no hesitation in his stride; obviously, then, he knew where I was hidden (I learned afterwards that he had watched me hide with the help of a pocket mirror he sometimes used for poker). He couldn't come at me from in front, for I covered the whole yard. But there was the wall, the one he knocked the chip out of firing at the bee. He could climb it—it was just there. I began to doubt the wisdom of my hiding-place. My heart beat faster. Just to heighten the excitement, I felt in my pocket for snap and cracked the ampoule under my nose, inhaling deeply. My heart duly swelled, my head thudded: every detail of the yard engraved itself in my brain. The light was twice as white and intense, the shadows . . . The shot cracked immediately beneath me and the bullet splintered the wooden door an inch from my head. Crazily leaning out, I saw Marchmare race along the wall at my feet and then dive at right angles across the yard into the big open garage and throw himself flat under the Bentley. I fired at him, but the shot went miles wide, scarring the garage wall.

It was a nice bit of work. Staring, I could just see a bump of shadow in the garage that the car didn't make. It might be his shoulder. But the target himself was safe, as long as I stayed where I was. I rose soundlessly and hurried to the trapdoor in the centre of the loft. Here a ladder ran down into the harness-room. Creeping down this inside the safety of the building, I walked through the harness-room and then through another door into a derelict room where my aunt used to organize her Girl Guides back in the 'twenties. This trip had taken me much closer to Marchmare. I could see the garage only ten yards away through the dusty panes. I edged up along the wall. Another shot crashed through the window and buried itself viciously in the wooden wall. A splinter droned solemnly over my head. Looking up startled, I saw how my shadow, thrown hugely across the ceiling, had given me away. Still, it was certain that he couldn't touch me from where he was. Straining my eyes into the deep shadow under the motor, I saw nothing for a moment. Then something bright winked and moved—the buckle on his shoe. I counted 'One . . . two . . .' and fired on three through the glass. It cut my face; the bullet went whe-e-e-e and then clanged metallically on the underside of the motor. I waited. Nothing happened. I don't know what I expected: perhaps that he would surrender. I looked at my watch. Time was nearly up.

As the hand came up to 12.45 I put the Parabellum down on the sill and cautiously walked outside with my hands in the air.

There was a cackle of glee under the motor. 'You surrendered, morrie! You surrendered!'

'I did nothing of the kind,' I said crossly. 'Time was up.'

'No, it wasn't.'

'Yes, it was.'

'Anyway,' I said, 'I thought I'd hit you.'

'*Hit* me? You couldn't hit a fly with its pants down.'

'Anyway,' I said lamely, 'nice shooting.'

At this moment a window high up in the house overlooking the yard opened. The mad face of my great-aunt appeared in it. Staring out blankly into space she cooed: 'Come on, children! L-u-u-u-nch-time!'

After lunch we cleaned the shooters in the gun-room and leisurely refought the battle over a whisky-and-soda. I felt a mild regret for the shot-up stableyard, but, as Marchmare said: 'It did make a top-loyal battleground'.

On the whole it had been a capital weekend, and when the time came to leave in the evening, to go on to Dover and catch the boat, everyone waved us goodbye from the doorstep and I felt more regret at leaving the fubbsy old place than I had done for years.

14

WE GOT through Customs O.K. at Dover. Being summer, there were lots of cars. You know the type, squares in one-piece caps and a lot of kids looking at Esso maps and yelling with excitement and Mum and Dad earnestly comparing the virtues of the afternoon with the evening boat. Several darling old A.A. men came up to us and looked very knowingly under the bonnet and checked the engine numbers. I had to look down not to laugh.

Still, I got that dodgy feeling waiting in the shed and thinking of the front we'd have to put on coming back through that great airy place with the ozone blowing through it and the scrubbed concrete floors.

The crossing was rather rough. We watched the square in the one-piece cap making unsteadily for the loo.

Why is one so pitiless with squares? I don't know how it is, but I can watch Colonel Bulbul taking the poor half-wide mugs for a right ride and never turn a hair. I suppose it's because the squares are the harmless does and we're the wolves. The does are the world's working force so they have to be protected. Maybe the people who conned them into being the way they are feel vaguely guilty and reckon the least they can do is provide the decent screen of law and civilization to veil their patient ten-quid-a-week sufferings. . . . I don't know. So the boys who work these poor squares to death have this way of making money out of them legit. O.K., so we have our methods of taking it away again.

Marchmare and I went down to the first-class saloon and bought a drink. The boat heaved as it left the harbour. We bought brandy. It was good and dead cheap—it was funny to think we drank the same stuff in London at four times the price.

But unfortunately I didn't enjoy it. Because now that we were off on the job (and now that it was too late to turn back) a feeling I'd had vaguely at the back of my mind and repressed sprang to life and became a conviction.

I had the certain feeling that something was wrong somewhere. I didn't feel scared. It wasn't that at all. I've got the knack for seizing a problem—when I want to—and grabbing the meat in it, and now several things struck me. First, what with the general excitement and the big stakes we were playing for, I had allowed myself to get pressured by Marchmare into taking off without securing my base—a fatal rule to break, 'specially if you're a deviator. Not that I blamed Marchmare; it'd been my own fault. Second, I got the trembles every time I remembered how I saw Plinth outside Winston's that night Mike and I were there. Funny . . . he'd made that remark about not going there because of Old Bill. Was *that* coincidence or had he let it slip? If he *had* . . . I've never known Plinth *ever* just *happen* to turn up somewhere right off his manor the one night a bit of deviation's being planned. I couldn't prove what was at the bottom of what had led him there—but the point was I hadn't even tried. If I'd stopped to think: that all by itself would have been an excellent reason for delaying the off. But I hadn't bothered.

So that left the biggest question mark (if there was anything in these ideas)—Mike. Come to think of it, we'd all three done a stupid thing. We'd trusted him. You don't trust deviators. You do business with them, which is different. But he'd been so convincing . . . that act in Winston's, if it was an act . . . again, I'd never stopped to think. If there's one fatal weakness in Marchmare's mental equipment it's his rosy optimism. One night I had a word with him about the whole deal and wanted to pull it to pieces from top to bottom. But he was too bored to talk about it.

'Oh, don't be so *silly*, morrie. Things never go wrong with *us*.'

But that's all cobblers. The worst of it all was, there was nothing definite. If there had been it would have been easy. I'd have just said no and stacked, even if there'd been a million at the end of it. But this was only instinct, like you have when you somehow know you're going to win or lose a game of five-card stud. Still, I forced Marchmare to listen, and we had a big row. He thought I was scared. The trouble with him is he's that much younger than I am and he lets his feelings run away with him. Once he's worked up for a deal and says yes to it there's no stopping him. But you must never do that. You don't gamble on all five cards, only on one. But I saw now how he'd pulled me along with him.

Sure, I liked Mike. But the little deviators like him, they crack. They squeal, maybe out of jealousy or because they imagine someone's trying to do them for their whack. They have woman trouble. They spend too much trying to make the scene with the big-income groups. Worst of all, as I said somewhere before, they all think they're too smart and that's when they get nicked . . . screwing or conning or going in for a bit of archbishop or knocking once too often, and then they get pinched and do bird, and often in the nick they get into despair and go potty and start making some funny friends. And that's when they grass.

And, yet again, there might be nothing in it. Just imagination. After all, deviation was always a gamble. Yes, but this was a very big gamble. The funny thing was, it wasn't Reisemann I worried about. He had to be straight up. Oh, no, the worry was all on the home ground, behind the lines, not in front, and I didn't like it if I was right—oh, not at all. I had the worst fit of willies in the biz, which is when you feel that the real deal isn't the one you're on, that you're being used as a front and being framed. I'd put it across enough people myself in my time. But now it was my turn. Then my thoughts turned to the commies, and what might happen if something went the other way and *they* smelled something and didn't trust *us*. My ideas slid towards bullets: the mounting tension and the moment you said to yourself *now*. The getting to one's feet and then the flat crash like a dirty word and then the pain which made you real with agony.

I looked over to where Marchmare was now sitting in the corner of the saloon. He had taken out a pack of cards and was playing solitaire. . . . He wore a lightweight suit of dark blue, a knitted tie from Fisher's, suède casuals, gold links. He crossed his knees like any Old Etonian waiting to take his mother out to lunch. Then the sun flamed for an instant and silhouetted him. The black shape was threatening, rigid and merciless. The sun died, and the remains of a wave crashed off the deck into the sea. Marchmare would never turn back.

'Morrie!' he shouted. 'Come over here! Play you gin rummy five quid a corner!'

'Not just for a minute,' I said.

He looked at me. 'Worried, dearie?'

'No,' I said. The storm was worse. Now all the poor goons were tottering into the heads and sicking their hearts out. I came to a decision there and then and that was good, because once you've decided you feel better, no matter what decision it is. I thought: 'Well, we'll play it off and hold tight and see what happens.' It wasn't much of a decision, but it was a lot better than none at all.

I went over and joined Marchmare now.

'I thought you were never coming,' he said. 'I watched you over there. Do you know what I think? I think you looked scared.'

'Oh, belt up,' I said, 'and deal, will you.'

He smiled, but his eyes were that dull agate colour, the way they always were if you crossed him.

'Well, but you were so silent, dearie,' he said.

'Morrie,' I said.

'What?'

It slipped out before I could stop it. 'There's something wrong with this deal.'

He blew up. 'What the bloody hell is it?' he raged. We were both on edge. 'There are times when I've *had* you. You're too finicky. You think too much. This is a game where you make your mind up and then go through with it. Finish. Do I have to draw you a tiny map?'

I was getting the needle and it could have turned into an ugly fight. There were a lot of glasses on the table and no one about but the barman, a fat Belgian with a cast in his eye.

'Well,' I said, 'let's keep calm about it.'

'Calm!' he shouted. 'What the hell's the matter with you? What I see in this deal is a tiny tiny risk, darling, and then a sixteen grand pay-off. In reddy. Tomorrow night. And now remember this,' he continued. 'You're not on your own this time, dearie. This isn't one of your lone-ranger tape-recorder jobs. This time there's other people to consider besides darling little morrie in his ickle mobcap and his ickle tiny candle and his ickle milk and biccies trotting up to his nice little cosy bed.' He was blazing.

'All right,' I said, 'I know.'

'Yellow streak down your back.'

Then we both burst out laughing and thank God it was over —yellow streak: it was too like that other time that day we were making for the Czech frontier, it seemed like yesterday. So we had it away smartly to the bar and noshed down two more brandies, and then a few more on top for luck, and by the time we'd downed them Ostend harbour was only a short spit off, so we unhooked ourselves from the bar and scarpered to look for the jam.

I don't know if you've ever been to Frankfurt; I hadn't before. Anyway, never go there—it's a dreadful manor.

'Let's check straight in at the Frankfurterhof,' said March-mare as we drove into the town.

This seemed an excellent idea. It was five in the evening, we had driven most of the day and we were beaten out.

The Frankfurterhof was a very proper gaff. An old kraut in a mulberry uniform and one of Göring's cast-off hats seized our suitcases and marched away with them. Our less kosher luggage was in our pockets.

As soon as we got into our room we locked the door against any intruders on a final game with the shooters. We emptied the magazines. In turn, one of us went into the loo and practised sniping on the other as he moved swiftly, crouching, between the beds and made a dive for the door. For better practice still, we drew down the venetian blinds and tried the whole thing over again in the half-dark. We threw ourselves flat on the floor twenty times on the word 'drop'. About halfway through this exercise we began to hear surprised American voices next door. We giggled helplessly. Marchmare . . . a passing shot from right to left.

'Like grouse, dearie,' he said.

We each filled a flask with the whisky we bought on the boat. It's useful to throw in an ice-cream's face and spoils his aim for that half-second. Finally, we played what we used to call 'stalking the boar at Passau'—a game where one of you had to wait in the loo and the other had to go in and kill you unarmed. Then, stripping naked, we did a lot of exercises and practised judo falls.

I wished the Archbubble's check call would come.

Just as I'd gone in to shower and the cold tap was full on over my head the phone went, and I heard Marchmare cop for it. A moment later I heard the click as he replaced it and his head appeared round the door.

'That was Reisemann,' he said. 'All as planned.'

I ran out of the shower, dripping. I dried myself and went over to my suitcase and opened it, pulling out clothes. I felt nervous, hearing my heart murmuring and bumping and watching my hands shaking. Then it was over, and I was dressing in nice, easy, loose clothes; I put on suède casuals—no laces to trip you up, stumble over. No loose threads, buttons. Coat left wide open in front and the Parabellum drops plonk in the pocket. You could fire straight through it. No time to draw if you're caught napping. Or else fire for diversion, I was thinking; I fire for the lamp and the geezer'll look away ten to one and Marchmare's got him—snap—in that flash of the exploding light. Now Marchmare's looking at his shooter, turning it over thoughtfully in his hands by the window—examine, shuffle the action, wipe, load, stow away. A quick drink next and a final check round the pad. Wipe everything clear of dabs in case we shan't be coming back. Now that everything's getting under way we're smooth, calm, methodical and easy-moving. Just one thing to wait for now, the Archbubble's check call.

Five minutes later the phone screams again briefly.

'*Zimmer neunzig*,' says Marchmare.

I hear the clack of the Archbubble's voice. 'Morrie?'

'Yes.'

'No Mike.'

'*What?*'

'I don't know what happened. Geezer never showed.'

Long pause.

'Oh.'

'What d'you want to do?' clattered the Archbubble. 'Keep going?'

'Sure,' said Marchmare. 'Keep going. Everything as arranged.'

'O.K. Good luck.'

'Good luck. Be seeing you.'

'Don't say it, morrie,' said Marchmare, without looking at me as we ran downstairs.

I felt blank inside, except for that loud murmuring of my heart. 'We'll have to hurry,' was all I said, 'or we'll be late for the meet.' We picked up our bent passports at reception and slipped into the darkness like a couple of ghosts. Marchmare called a taxi and we hustled into it.

'Hauptbahnhof,' I said, and we were off on the first leg of a long haul. From the speeding cab Frankfurt looked really drab, even at night; that horrible kraut neon, too white, too green. We passed several cafés and spotted people noshing and stretching themselves and drinking. Lucky them. I wished we were

just going to nosh too. I made my thoughts dwell on the nosh
I would have with Marchmare afterwards, though it wasn't
easy. And then? Who knows? Mexico, maybe. And perhaps
Christice, too. It'd be nice. Retire, even. Laze in the sun, maybe
write a book or something. No more angst. Even a long charver
with Mrs. Marengo would be all right. Funny how one felt like
that just *before*. I began to sweat into my shirt and soon it was
sticking to my back in the muggy warmth. I began to think
about the trip home. Jesus, there was a long road in front of us
—we were really earning our money this time. Home. One
didn't have a home, really. Tumbledown wasn't exactly a *home*.

I looked back. Was the Archbubble tailing our cab? I saw a
low pair of sidelights dancing on the road. The car was white
and—yes—it was an XK. *What had happened to Mike?* The Archbubble must have gone potty when he didn't show. Well, I
thought, it's just too bad. I glanced at Marchmare. He was
sitting very still, watching the floor. We'd agreed not to speak—
no point in giving the driver anything to remember. You never
really knew. Cab-drivers at home were mostly grasses and there
was no reason to suppose they'd be any different here. What
was kraut law like? Silly question. That nice charver, now . . .
doubtless Mrs. Marengo was heavily engaged with the man from
Eire this very minute. The cab, a Mercedes, jarred over tram-
lines and cobbles and swerved to the right. Marchmare ducked
sharply. But we were only at the station.

We got out, not too much on the hurry-up, and I paid the
man off slowly, looking round to see if I could spot the Archbubble. But I couldn't. Probably a good thing. The street was
wide, and on the other side there were a group of sidestreets;
he would be parked in one of those, waiting for us to leave
again. But it would have been reassuring to see him. I looked
about for the main cab-rank but Marchmare had already seen
it and I followed him off to the left. We walked rather slowly,
close to the wall of the main station block. There was no one
much about. People were still eating. As we came close to the
line of shiny cabs we slowed to a dawdle. I counted them: one

. . . two . . . three. The rear door of the third one opened a crack. I was surprised. Somehow I never thought it would really happen. It was a very ordinary cab, a dirty black Kapitan. We made as if to walk past it, then we turned and peered in at the driver.

'Get in,' said a voice from the back seat. Its English was quite good.

'Get in the back,' said the voice.

I did as it said. Marchmare got in the front seat.

'Both in the back,' said the voice irritably.

'Not on your nellie,' snapped Marchmare, and slammed his door. Maybe the kraut wasn't quite up to our argot, but as the car set off a street-lamp lit up the corner of his face, which was twisted with crossness. The main thing was to make the kraut look small from the word go. Reduce him to size. After all, we were armed too. Marchmare and I started chatting the ice-cream up.

'A fine night,' I said, thinking, well, one's got to start somewhere.

'For an H bomb,' added Marchmare. Now that the attack whistle had gone we both felt much better.

The kraut said nothing, but his face was still rumpled with anger. It was not a nice face, and it had a green hat laced with a little green cord perched on top of it. The vast bulky body was swathed in a green overcoat. The torpedo who was driving smelled strongly of weinbrand, like a still. He was outsize and he looked disloyal too, I decided. I wondered if they were *real* commies. You know how it is, everyone in the U.K. talks about them with bated breath and they acquire some sort of mystique, and then when you see them close to they're just ordinary ice-creams and mostly they're not too clean. So with this pair. Now that we had actually embarked on this biz it all began to look dimly *Thirty-nine Steps*, because it's the tension of not knowing what to expect—a broken arm, maybe—that makes you nervy beforehand; but once you're off it's generally better, especially if you've got off to a thumping good start.

Marchmare put his tongue out at me. We began giggling. The krauts said nothing. It was fun, now: heady, like the first glass of Krug 53.

'Do you play five-card stud?' said Marchmare suddenly.

'No,' snapped the geezer beside me. I decided he must definitely be a commie. I was prepared to hate the commies from that moment. For the first time in my life I felt patriotic. They were so *square*. I was getting the needle because they didn't do or say anything, or tell us where we were going. I looked out at the scenery but I couldn't make any sense of it. I saw a few tight little kraut houses and huge, well-tilled fields appeared in the lights of the jam. We were nowhere near the autobahn which we had left at the end of the town; we were nipping down a secondary road which the Kapitan was making heavy work of. Marchmare, who is never very good in jamjars, said he felt sick. I thought, 'It's fun, it's fun,' like a kid. Like a kid, too, I was willing myself to make it fun.

Then something happened. A gun appeared in the hand of the kraut next to me. It looked very workmanlike.

'You will now be searched,' he said.

There was no time to be scared. I was stroking my chin as he spoke, revolving my deep thoughts, so I simply let my hand continue leftwards, putting everything I had behind it and straightening it. I hit him in the throat with the percussion edge. Considering the cramped quarters, I hit him very hard. He gagged, making the strangest noise, then there was a huge report and I felt like a fly when a soda bottle's opened in its face, but the bullet went straight through the door of the car, tearing a hole the size of a small ham in the metal. It must have been a dumdum.

He didn't have time to shoot again. Before the driver could move it was all over. I broke the kraut's wrist expertly, which made him scream, then I hit him over the nose with his own gun to make him shut up. I have no time for dumdums. If he'd hit me he'd have splashed my guts over the motor and it'd've made an abattoir look tidy.

134

'Stop the motor,' I said to the driver in English, not caring whether he understood or not. I was cold. I would have shot him on the spot. But Marchmare had already leaned over and switched off the ignition key, pulling it out and pocketing it. As the car slowed, he put the brake on.

'*Raus*,' I said to the driver, opening the door. He stumbled out and stood on the verge. For a commie, he looked very numbed, woebegone and afraid.

'It wasn't your fault,' Marchmare said to him in his most maddening voice. 'Your mate should've stopped the motor before he did that. I can't think what you were up to.'

The XK swept up, dimming its lights. The window wound down and the Archbubble's face appeared. 'On,' I muttered to him, 'or we'll attract attention. Stop up the road.' The Archbubble trod on it and was gone. The road was straight here, and I saw his brake lights wink as he parked a long way further up.

There was no time to lose.

'Reisemann,' I said to the driver. '*Wo ist?*'

The kraut was silent, looking from one to the other of us. Marchmare stepped up and smacked him twice.

'*Antworten.*'

Nothing. This could have gone on all night, and we hadn't that kind of time. Any minute someone—the law—could patrol past and see the Kapitan with that hole in it.

'I'll search him,' I said to Marchmare. I went up to do this and the oafo made some bumbling effort to get me between Marchmare and himself. I lost my temper and put a horrible armlock on him. Then I took the tip of his little finger and held it gently, squeezing it with the ball of my thumb. He was rather a small man.

'One joint at a time,' I said.

'*Wass?*'

'I'll break you in pieces,' I said savagely. '*Cassez.*' I didn't know the kraut for it.

'Schloss Kassburg,' he said then, obviously hating himself for it. 'Four kilometres.'

'Thanks,' I said, and Marchmare felled him like an ox with his own shooter. I went over to the car and tipped the busted kraut out into the ditch. Then I took my socks off and put them on over my hands before I handled their jam at all. Marchmare produced the key. I let in the clutch and took a last lamp at the scene. It was a nice night, but damp. The kraut who'd been too free with his dumdums was just coming round and beginning to cry with pain.

We drove off down the road to where the Archbubble was waiting.

We found Schloss Kassburg on the Archbubble's ordnance map by the light of a torch. In the light of the aggravation we'd just had we had to reshuffle the plan.

'We can use the two motors,' I said to the Archbubble. 'We two'll go in with the Kapitan. You follow with your lights out so's they don't sus you. Keep your distance. Hang about. If we're not out of the gaff in say thirty minutes come belting in after us.'

'If you can,' giggled Marchmare.

'If it goes the other way,' I said, 'we'll grab the merchandise and try and pass it to you. What you do with it's your own affair.'

'Oi don't like it,' grumbled the Archbubble.

'You won't regret it, dolling,' I said, and Marchmare bent double, laughing.

'By the way,' I said, 'what happened to Mike, while we're at it?'

'I don't know,' said the Archbubble. 'I never had time to find out, did I?'

'Did he leave England?' said Marchmare.

'No, he never,' said the Archbubble, 'because I had his exes and ticket all ready for him and he never collected them. I mean that's not like a deviator not to pick up his exes, is it?'

'It all looks very dodgy to me,' I said.

But what could we do? It was just a terrible thing.

We said a fond Greek farewell to the Archbubble, got back in our respective jams and set off, Marchmare map-reading. As he's the worst map-reader in Europe it was a lucky thing Kassburg wasn't hard to find. After about five minutes' driving a big block of masonry looked up sharply on the skyline. Slowing, we saw a narrow lane dipping off the metalled high road and took it. The lane was deep in mud. The Kapitan groaned on its worn axles. In places the lane was hopelessly overgrown and was far too narrow. The surface was ruinous and very few cars seemed to have used it. The wheels whined and spun on the grass. It would be a bad place to come back along quick.

I was still trying to work out what sort of angst the pair we'd left behind might have arranged when it was on top of us. A geezer sprang into our lights waving a shooter. He went straight to the rear door of the Kapitan.

But I had thoughtfully locked this. I once had a bankruptcy writ served on me in a traffic jam, and I automatically distrust unlocked doors. So the torpedo waded back to me and I wound down the window a crack. He got his fingers in and tried to push the window all the way down, so I rapped him over the knuckles rather sharply with the Parabellum.

He swore loudly. 'Where are the others?' he shouted angrily in the serviceable, heavily accented English they all seemed to speak.

Marchmare leaned over. 'Must we hold the post-mortem here?' he said. 'The point is we're here and so's their poxy motor. What more do you want?'

'A huge great drink,' I said, and we both giggled.

'I am to get in,' said the torpedo with arrogant fury.

'Then ask nicely, sweetheart,' I snapped, and was ready to shoot.

There was a moment's extreme tension, then Marchmare reached back, opened his own door, slipped out and went round the back. The kraut gawped when he saw the shooter in Marchmare's hand. As he got in the back with Marchmare beside him I turned and said to the kraut: 'I'll have that,' because driving with an unfriendly shooter in the back of one's neck makes me nervous, and when he handed it over I opened the window and threw it out into the bushes.

'That's right,' said Marchmare politely, 'we've had one battle down to shooters already and we don't want another.'

'Goodness,' I said mildly, 'if it's all as easy as this we haven't a thing to worry about.' I let in the clutch. 'How far from here?' I said to the kraut.

'Half a kilometre. . . . I understand yet not nothing.'

'Ah,' said Marchmare kindly, 'but that's probably not your job.'

'Where are the others?' said the kraut again, sullenly.

'A little argument happened,' said Marchmare. 'But they can just about walk.'

'Here we are,' I said, 'this must be it,' for I could see an extraordinary building, far stranger than Tumbledown, surging up out of the darkness in our path. It was gigantic: it looked like the Tower of London, only spread out to cool like rice-pudding—a tangled chaos of turrets, clocks and broken windows, and on the wall above the keep the kraut motioned us to drive through glimmered an aged kraut motto lit by the lamp above.

It did not prepare me for what happened next. There was a hiss and a flash and a dazzling searchlight shone flat in my face and blinded me. Like a fool, I spun the wheel to get away from that murdering brilliance and the motor clanged into the wall. I hit my knee on the dashboard, the motor cut and Marchmare and I were flung in a heap.

'Kurt! Kurt!' screamed a voice, and I saw our passenger dive for the door and fling himself out and beyond.

'*Raus!*' shouted the voice, again hysterically. '*Raus!*'

But I sat there for that one vital moment; the suddenness of the light stunned me—and then a huge hammering noise started up—it felt as if it was in my head—above which I heard the brilliant bang of a tyre bursting and the car was jumping and shaking as the great bullets clobbered it. . . . 'Christ,' I thought, 'every one of the bastards have hit me.' I looked at Marchmare, but somehow he was away out of it, a narrow white shirtfront spreadeagled against the wall with his hands in the air. I tried to follow, but was only halfway when the remains of the windscreen disintegrated into my seat. Bullets went high and low again like a mad little game of cincinnatti, screaming off the brickwork around us and the car roof. Then in a lull I moved like a dart, swallowing my terror and joining him against the wall and sticking my hands up too, you *bet*, and now there we were lit up by that light with no more cover than two fleas on the side of a tumbler. And I wasn't even scratched and I thought: 'Oh, well, that's something.'

If it was all designed to cut me down to size—well, I was cut down to size.

'Hurt?' I said to Marchmare. He shook his head, but he can only have meant not much, for blood was dribbling down his sleeve and forming irregular black splashes on the cobbles. I cautiously got out my handkerchief and handed it to him, half-expecting some more of the leaden treatment, but nothing happened. Marchmare pulled his sleeve back exposing his wrist. It was a long thin cut, but deep. It might have been glass, or a splinter, but not a bullet wound. He started to bind it up. We stood there side by side like a couple of spies. I never want to get closer to that firing-squad feeling. My heart was hammering now like the action of that machine-gun, and my head rang like a cathedral after the deafening noise and now with the silence that followed it. I thought: 'Hell, you can't fire machine-guns like that even in the middle of krautland without someone wanting to know about it'—but even as I spoke more firing started, incredibly, somewhere to the east, about a mile away; and I realized it must be an army tank range with maybe a division on a night-firing exercise, which was very clever.

In the courtyard the enemy sat behind their light watching us. Staring even anywhere near it you could see nothing, but now I heard footsteps nearing us, ringing on the flags. Then a hand dropped on my shoulder, yanking me forward as if I were a toy and ripping the cloth. Another hand grabbed Marchmare and banged our heads together. A flood of stars shot through me—but it was nothing to the rage and humiliation—and then we were being kicked and pushed through a doorway which was dark by this giant and the other kraut we had so kindly given a lift to. We found ourselves in a narrow ruinous hall covered in the dust of ages, the whole scene lit by a single weak bulb hanging over a broken-down staircase. To my left I saw a big room whose ceiling vanished in the gloom; there was a huge hole in the wall. The war? Or had the tanks used it as a target?

I turned to look at Marchmare, who looked green, though he managed a wink. A torrent of questions was pouring through my brain. How to get out? How to get Marchmare out with his dodgy arm? What had the Archbubble made of the scene? What were we to do with no shooters and no jamjar? I began to see what a lousy job we had made of the whole enterprise. And they had been clever . . . or had we been particularly stupid? Well, if you took the view that the whole expedition was stupid then the answer was yes. Still, under the circumstances, things could hardly have worked out otherwise; a lot of deviators might never have thought to bring shooters at all, and where would we have been without them? Trussed up like a couple of chickens and topped? Maybe that would happen anyway. Ought we to have let the two krauts search us back at square one? No, you didn't take that kind of treatment.

As we were pushed up the stairs I began to wonder who these people really were. This, too, was a new and equally unpleasant train of thought. Was there in fact any slush at all? After all, with Mike bent, the whole thing could be a gigantic con trick . . . nothing more . . . *and we had fallen*. But with what point? Where did Plinth fit in? But I had been over all that before. There was nothing to do now but play it out. But whenever I thought of Mike I had a pang of elemental hatred—and fear, too. I wondered if either of us had very long to live. And if there wasn't any slush what was the racket so sweetly run by these people who certainly *existed*, I thought, as the giant behind me put the leather in to get me up the stairs faster. There was only one certain thing: they were saving us for an interview with their Mr. Cream. Otherwise they'd have topped us with the spandau at the gate.

They halted us in front of an iron-studded door in a long passage. Once upon a time it might have been a rather kosher door, but it now looked very beaten over the hocks. The whole gaff gave off a nasty mouldy smell, and a little light edged along from another bulb over a broken window at the end. Then those huge hands grabbed us again and spun us to face the wall like a couple of naughty little boys being stood in the corner by Nanny. I got the dead needle. Looking sideways at Marchmare I could see that he had brightened up too. His arm had stopped bleeding.

It was good to have him there.

You never really knew with Marchmare.

There had been that big fight in Paris where it looked as if he were beaten right out and then, just as the hoods were lifting him out by the armpits to do him over properly in the street, he'd outed a knife and kicked one ice-cream in the hampsteads so you could hardly see where his mouth had been.

Maybe he'd pull a stroke now and, oh boy, did we need one with me all butterflies and wouldn't *you* have been?

Still, I thought, facing the wall with that nasty itch in my back which wanted to be where my face was, think what would happen when the slag picked up their linens in the King's Road the day the story broke, as it soon would. A rumour'd go over the vine and the burned-out debs turned punters' molls and press narks would get to hear about it and before you could say William Hickey in two languages every reporter on the Street'd be flooding Europe looking for us. Soon it would be July and August, annual slack period for the linens and everyone'd be spouting everything they knew about us like disloyal people always do: where we drank, where our dodgy property companies were, who our friends were—it was only a matter of time

141

before they got on to Christice, and what *would* Lord Chrism say?

I smiled and the giant, who was standing beside us, gave me a wack over the boat for it. More and more I wondered if we weren't simply going to be topped. After all, why not? 'Specially if Mike had been a grass all along and they figured we'd been bending the deal we'd be no use to them kicking—we could go flying out into the wide skies and sing and sing. And one-handed the Archbubble wouldn't get us out in a month of Woolworth sale-days. They'd probably just make sure we weren't law and quietly rub us out. Or maybe loudly, with the spandau. After all, they were krauts, weren't they? I hoped they'd aim high, not low. I didn't fancy the idea of it breaking my legs first.

I was aware that our two guards had separated; the giant was still watching us, but our ex-passenger had moishered over to the door and was holding a whispered rabbit with someone inside. I made up my mind to bluff it out. If I could. Maybe the enemy hadn't as many wild cards in the hole as I thought. There was only one way to find out—raise him with all the loot I hadn't got and then call him, and maybe that was the last thing I'd ever do.

The rabbiting at the door stopped. The steps came up from behind. I wondered if there was a shooter eyeing me between the shoulders. This is it, then, I thought, hackneyedly. Sure enough, we were grabbed again, spun round; the door opened from inside and we were shot through it like a couple of cricket balls.

15

ABALD, pot-bellied geezer of about fifty sat behind a kitchen table at the end of a dingy room—and Christ, if the ice-cream now didn't have the cheek to make noises like *surprise* when he saw us, as if we were a couple of seedy applicants for jobs with the mob who'd come in without knocking. There was a moment's awkward pause while the two torpedoes sidled in after us and locked the door while Marchmare and I and Reisemann stared at each other like incompatible people who've been ditched together at a cocktail party. Then something happened to me like inspiration and I doubled up and began to laugh and laugh until the tears came. The torpedoes looked puzzled and cross, like krauts do when there's any mirth flying about.

'Shut up!' shouted Reisemann. He said it in a broad Yorkshire accent and that stopped me because it stunned me. But then Marchmare and I looked at each other and of course we began to laugh some more. Best of all, I could see him cottoning to the line I was going to play. . . . Still, it was genuine too: quite often at snap parties you get this sort of thing happening—after you've had, say, five ampoules and you feel your head swelling like a balloon glass and your heart going like the hammers—you lamp someone, maybe it's a stranger, and you get the feeling you've got to laugh so strong that it's ludicrous and you just let it out because you'd burst otherwise—which is the whole point about snap, I suppose: you just don't give a damn.

And laughter like that spreads at snap parties till the gaff's filled with the roar of voices and drinking and glasses breaking and ampoules snapping and over it all this insane laughter, and presently some geezer starts undressing or a fat man goes off on a transvestite kick and comes down wearing Mrs. Marengo's floppy hat and doing a Spanish dance on greasy old scotches. But if (as happened to me one night at Mrs. Marengo's) there's a person there who hasn't been taking it you can get a nasty situation and you want to watch out, when and if you get snapped up for the first time, that you don't hand out too much aggravation and get yourself well thumped. With me and Mrs. Marengo that night I happened to come in on her when I was well snapped and she was entertaining the Man from Eire. I'd meant to tap her for the usual score but it ended up with a fearful screaming match because I wanted the Man from Eire to beat her and at the death that person screamed loudest of all and gave me a right bump.

And Reisemann came to this situation dead cold too. After all, he hadn't had the lights scared half out of him with a hail of machine-gun bullets, he hadn't been breaking wrists and getting shooters away from angry krauts. And it was obvious, too, that he was playing it from the snob angle—he thought he was king of Schloss Kassburg—and a rotten old gaff it was to be king of, too.

'Right-o, then,' said Reisemann, 'you can sit down when you've finished.'

He tried to keep his voice superior and too-good-for-you, but that's a morrie's favourite game, isn't it? Still, now wasn't the moment to be uppity, so we sat down while the torpedoes fiddled with their shooters.

Marchmare crossed his legs.

I did up what was left of my coat.

'You can smoke,' said Reisemann.

We lit up without showing all that much gratitude. 'Well,' I thought, 'so the condemned man had a smoke.' It was time to steam in, so I opened the batting.

'Well,' I snapped, 'perhaps you'll tell me what all this fooling's down to.' It was a very dangerous line, but it had to be.

Reisemann put his head on one side and opened his eyes as far as they would go. I soon found out this was a mannerism of his. They were extraordinary big eyes and dark brown with huge whites. They had a knack of never turning once they were on you, which wasn't at all nice.

'Fooling?' he repeated sharply.

'Yes,' I said. 'All this cobblers with shooters, machine-guns and kraut heavies. It's worse than a telly commercial.'

'Let me tell you——' Reisemann started.

I cut him short, though my shoulder-blades wriggled again. 'No, mister,' I said shortly. 'We're not interested in hearing things from you. What I want, before we get down to business——'

'If there is any business,' Marchmare put in.

'Is the answer to a few questions,' I said.

'You've had your first,' said Marchmare, neatly catching the ball. 'Why all the bowery moves?'

'I received a call from the man you so stupidly wounded——'

But we weren't going to let him get a word in edgeways.

'Look,' I said roughly, 'I told you, I couldn't care less about the pros and cons. We hurt your boy because he played it wrong. He's lucky we never topped him. As for the machine-guns and your frighteners handing out wacks and aggravation, all you managed to do was to shoot up your own motor.'

It worked. I thought he'd go potty. 'Listen!' he screamed, banging the table. 'I'm doing the talking here.'

'But you're not,' said Marchmare. The words ripped out of him like a burst from the spandau.

'We're all supposed to be deviators in this room,' I said, 'but as far as I can see you're not too clever at it.'

If he'd been going to he'd have shot us then, but he didn't. I remember wondering why not.

'If you've got a deal,' said Marchmare, 'now would be your time to start talking. Otherwise we've got a plane to catch.'

And we stood up. It was the nastiest thing we'd attempted, but it was psychology again. It had to be, though the giant was right up against me, one of the ugliest torpedoes I've ever seen, and huge, huge, his great hand like a ham against my chest, waiting to throw me over the back of the chair or break my neck, according to orders.

But no orders came.

'Business,' sneered Reisemann. 'Why should I do business with you?'

But he was *talking* it, wasn't he? And we were going to be like the ice-cream at the interview where the millionaire throws him a stone and says okay, mac, now sell me this for two grand.

'If you weren't satisfied who we were,' said Marchmare, 'why did you have your boys pick us up at the station anyway?'

He didn't answer. It was all very intriguing even if it didn't make sense. I stretched and yawned. 'Anyone got a drink?' I said. 'It's been a dry evening so far.'

It was an indication of the improving temperature when Reisemann nodded to the heavy, who lumbered off to the back of the drum and came back with a bottle. Marchmare snatched it and we both had a good belt at it. It was the cheapest wein-brand you could buy but, oh boy, it was good. And somehow most of the tension had slipped away.

'You know,' said Reisemann suddenly, 'you're quick. Very few would have got as far as you have this evening. I liked the way you handled my men. We did not intend to shoot you downstairs.'

'Oh, no, of course not,' I jeered.

'It was psychology,' said Reisemann seriously. And with a pinched smile: 'And the Kapitan was stolen on my instructions. So, you see, it is no loss to us.'

His East Riding accent grew less pronounced and he dropped back into the typical colourless English I suppose they teach them over there. But once upon a time I guessed that accent had been perfect. I wondered why. I also guessed he had been a spy, first for the Nazis. He impressed me as a very proper operator. Borrowing Kassburg for the evening had been a right stroke, on the edge of the army range.

'My arm hurts like hell,' grumbled Marchmare, 'thanks to your bloody firing-squad.'

'I'll get it fixed.'

'Ah, bollox,' said Marchmare. It was a good thing to say. It went home.

No. Reisemann wasn't an ordinary deviator. His job was at once more dangerous and less so than, say, Mr. Cream's, or Colonel Bulbul, or even a two-bit little bastard like Mike. All he had to do was sit there and plan.

But he also had to worry about the big boys at home.

'O.K.,' said Reisemann now, leaning forward, 'you say you know all about this business.'

'All we know is what we heard from our London contact.'

'Whose name is?'

'Mike.'

'Well,' said Reisemann, 'that's correct.'

'Christ,' I said impatiently, 'this is worse than the head-master's Greek grammar paper.'

'I've got to be sure,' said Reisemann. There was a little shadow on his face. That would be the boys at home. It must be funny, not trusting anyone, *ever*. A strain. He paused, then smiled and threw something on the table that he took from his pocket. 'Have a look,' he invited.

We craned over it. It was a photograph, rather smudged, of myself and Marchmare sitting in Winston's. I remembered now I'd seen a photoflood flash near me. We looked terrible, as drunk as hell. It was taken just after Mike had left me. In the gloom at the back sat the shapeless bulk of the Archbubble. Really! Not even Winston's was safe nowadays.

'Pretty good,' I said.

'Oh, yes,' said Reisemann proudly, 'there's nothing wrong with our information service; that was developed and on my desk six hours after it was taken.' He expanded. 'I also have your full dossiers—your ages, dates and places of birth—and I have your full family history on both sides for three generations back. We are very thorough.' He smiled. 'I am also satisfied that you are—deviators.'

'Oh, hooray!' said Marchmare.

'One question if I may: what made you turn criminal?'

But, as I remarked way back, if we could have answered *that* question we'd have been worth a degree in sociology anywhere. So we very properly stayed stumm.

Reisemann shrugged, smiling. 'It doesn't matter,' he said. 'But tell me . . . is your country really in such a state? Is it truly the pass to which your magnificent Western civilization has brought you that you, the scions of good houses, would turn traitor to a foreign power for a few pounds?'

Well, of course, we both nodded solemnly. Quite apart from the fact that that was indeed a perfectly accurate description of what we were doing, the question was a trap. To have indicated in any way at all that we weren't up to going the full belt, that we might grass, could still send things the other way. We had to be entirely ruthless; not to be could mean a drilling. What we were doing was very dangerous. It was like holding a grenade with the pin half out. It was far and away the most dangerous thing I'd ever tackled in my life.

Anyway, the ice-cream was wrong. It *wasn't* for a few pounds. We were into him for sixty grand, and that's a hell of a lot of loot by any standards.

'In any case,' Marchmare was saying, 'that hardly goes in the contract, does it?'

'Of course not,' said Reisemann equably, with those brown eyes right into him. 'It's just an interesting reflection to add to the store from which I assess the Western situation.'

No, Herr Reisemann was not like an ordinary deviator at all. 'Besides,' he was saying, 'you two model citizens would hardly set yourselves in judgement over us.'

'No,' I said promptly. 'As far as I'm concerned I'm on a job. As long as I get paid that's all I care about.'

All at once Reisemann looked more sinister than I had so far seen him. 'And a very healthy attitude, *liebkind*,' he said, 'but that is not quite the end of the affair. You realize that until you have handed over the merchandise to your contact in England you will be closely watched?'

'Watch away,' said Marchmare. 'We shan't knock you.'

'Even,' pursued Reisemann, 'if you were in the hands of the police and decided to—to . . .'

'Grass,' supplied Marchmare.

'Thank you . . . yes . . . there would eventually be an accident with a truck.'

'Oh, hell, yes,' I said placidly. 'In our circles that would happen anyway if the job were big enough and someone grassed.'

Reisemann smiled his widest so far, and it wasn't very wide. 'You are good boys,' he nodded approvingly. 'Yes, yes . . . you have never fought in any wars?'

'Not till tonight,' said Marchmare feelingly.

'Well, you have nerve,' said Reisemann.

'You'll give us the business, then?' said Marchmare, beginning to get restive. After all, that was the main thing.

'In a minute, yes. But first I have another proposition to put to you.'

'Another one?' I said.

'Yes,' said Reisemann. He summed us up for a moment and said: 'You know we have already some of your compatriots in our network.'

Oh, so it was *that*.

'Yes,' said Marchmare, 'but with our publicity——'

'You wouldn't remain in England,' said Reisemann.

Marchmare looked at me. 'I wonder what their bird's like, morrie.'

'We could teach it to dress better, anyway,' I said. 'The ones I've seen look the most ghastly old boilers.'

'Exactly,' said Reisemann. 'I will come to that. Meanwhile, you have good brains. You are daring. No patriotism—at least, not yet. Yes, you could be useful.'

Yes, I thought, already working out how we could be double agents and cop for a two-way whack. I sat watching him anticipating his gold medal back home for pulling a stroke like roping us in.

'You would have your own flat,' said Reisemann. 'And you would be well paid. The equivalent of ten thousand pounds a year to spend.'

'And the work?' I said.

'You will have two tasks,' said Reisemann immediately. 'First, training our men to work in England. Second, broad-casting to your truck-drivers over our networks at night. You see,' he said, studying his nails, 'you are both a very rare type. You are both high-born, *hochgeboren*.' He spat the word. 'But this is useful to us, for you can train men for work in high places. Women, too. You are traitors. With you on our staff a great deal could be achieved. You could teach accent, clothes, how to behave in big houses, nightclubs, at large parties. We would rebuild your Winston's for you, perhaps your school....'

I wondered how they would set about rebuilding Bruce Brace and nearly giggled, but it was tempting. Plenty of money, good food, a new Bentley—English clothes smuggled through the diplomatic bag, never a backward glance at the law again ... provided we behaved.

'Just this mission,' Reisemann was saying, 'and then one night you would disappear. A nine-day wonder in the papers—and you would finish your days with us.'

I hoped there would be plenty of them; still, I was *severely* tempted. For of course the ice-cream was right: the time would surely come—and it might be any day now—when the three of us had to get our collars felt. Talking of the Archbubble ...

'Yes,' said Reisemann, reading my thoughts, 'I'll take the Greek. Well? What do you say?'

'I'll think about it,' I said, 'and let you know after this deal. I'll certainly think about it.' After all, it was nice to be appreciated.

'I'll think about it too,' said Marchmare. We looked at each other. Of course the three of us would go if we went at all, I thought. I couldn't see into the future then. It was a strange variation on the three musketeers. Thinking of the Archbubble put me on still another track.

'By the way,' I said to Reisemann suddenly, 'do you trust Mike?'

'Of course not,' he said.

'We think he's grassed,' said Marchmare.

'Ah,' said Reisemann fondly, 'well I *know* he has. I had the news this morning. He was picked up by the police at lunchtime yesterday and he told them all he knew. He will be attended to.' He picked gently at one nail. 'That is why you now have an extremely difficult and dangerous mission ahead of you. Do you still wish to continue?'

'Yes,' I said.

'Yes,' said Marchmare. To me he said: 'I'm sorry, morrie. You were dead right.' His eyes had gone that peculiar agate shade that they went when he wanted to have sex or kill. One way and another Mike was already dead.

'In that case,' said Reisemann, 'I have thirty thousand pounds for you.' He opened a drawer and produced a huge mass of notes. He smiled very slightly. 'These notes are good. They are West German marks. You will bank them in Geneva if you are sensible, I think, in a numbered account.'

Then he picked up an attaché case from the floor, snapped back the catches and showed us the slush. It was all there in those nearly perfect notes like the one Mike had shown me, a quarter of a million quid of it.

Back at the hotel we changed our plan. Sitting over champagne back in Room 90 at the Frankfurterhof we agreed with the Archbubble that he could have the dodgy job of taking the slush back to the U.K. That was the advantage of his having reached Germany by a different route. The safest thing would have been to stash the slush and wait till the angst cooled, but Reisemann wouldn't wear that—unless we refunded our loot.

There wasn't any question of that, was there? so we agreed to pressure the Archbubble into making the switch—apart from anything else he'd had a quiet night hanging about outside Kassburg, while Marchmare and I were decidedly in need of a rest. So we reserved for ourselves the kosher job of taking the marks down to Geneva and banking them, also a nice quiet day maybe picking up a new wristwatch. Hell, we'd worked for it.

I spent a long time with them working out the odds, and we reckoned that by and large the Archbubble had a better than sporting chance. For one thing if the law knew from Mike that we were in Frankfurt you'd have expected them to get busy, but we'd had the obbs out very carefully all morning and there wasn't a sign of them so far.

Looking at it one way the point was that Mike had lots of form. He'd done more bird than I'd had hot dinners. He had no imagination and, as we'd seen, he hadn't the guts to play the game for the big money. The law could buy him for a pony—and, for all his rabbiting about a punch-up, when it came to a rub in that little granite room at the back of the nick he'd take their cash not their wacks. Next, what could he really tell the law when it came to it? And how much importance would Old Bill attach to what he said with all that form behind him? Well, quite a lot, obviously: enough to make them sus like mad. It would go straight to the Yard and Old Bill would check to see if we were in the country and they'd immediately discover we weren't—in fact, they'd know that *now*. But, as I've said, the law had never had anything concrete on any of us; officially we were just three dodgy layabouts and no one really knew how we made our loot—they just sussed it was all bent. Again, the slag was always running screaming to the law about us with the idea of making a beehive to spend in the Sharkham; the whole contents of the Sharkham practically was Press-cum-coppers' nark slag who thought they knew it all. But the law, having done quite a lot of the taxpayers' loot on them already, had discovered long ago that only a twentieth of what the slag had to tell was worth a rub; ninety per cent of it was all cobblers. So, I thought, let Mike grass to the wide skies—what could he actually say? That is, without putting himself in the nick—and I remembered his telling me that his next stretch would be seven-to-ten c.t. Again, the law would want to know how he'd found out all this about the slush. He could say he'd overheard it all in a nightclub, but Old Bill wouldn't wear that. Come to a rub, would they get all agitated when they'd rabbited with him and apply for warrants on pure sus and be waiting for us at Dover? My guess was that they wouldn't—not until they had something better to go on than cobblers from an oafo like him, anyway.

If we were right—*if*—the Archbubble could make it back to the U.K. with the merchandise with a reasonably good margin on the odds, and then he could deliver it, cop for the other half of our whack of loot and the contact could sit on it until he thought it was safe to pass it to the distributors. We'd have done our work.

But there was another way of looking at it too, and, being a born doubter it hadn't escaped me. It was a possibility so terrible that no one could have voiced it anyway, so I'll never know if either of the others thought of it too or not. This was to assume that Mike had been working for the law all along, that it was the *law* who'd originally intercepted that beehive and passed it to Mike to pass to us because then they'd make a double killing. Plinth and his boys had had a bellyfull of us and if their little plan worked they could put us away for a three bottom weight *and* round up the slush with Interpol all in one nice easy movement. . . . Didn't I say somewhere how you had to watch Old Bill because, though he was usually a groove behind, sometimes all unexpected he'd be one in front? In that case Mike was a brave little character with a lot of guts, because we'd have quietly killed the ice-cream if we'd ever sussed him and he was taking a big big chance with his blag on my never checking on the Irish, Phelps, which I certainly never had. . . . And if I was right we were properly soldered right into that little grey home they've got on the Moor whatever we did

. . . so there was no question of going back and no point much in going on, except that we had to go on because life just never stops and you never know, there might be a chance somewhere if Old Bill slipped, which he does sometimes, believe it or not. But we were surrounded and cut off *if* I was right and it didn't matter what we did—we were clobbered any way up.

And that made Reisemann's promise of asylum more and more attractive, especially if one thought too much about the interior of the Yard and the funny things they sometimes did to you while they got the *details* right, or being on remand at Brixton, or, after that, looking into the grey years ahead. . . . But even if I was right I somehow felt I could never never say it to Marchmare or the Archbubble: after all, what was the point? *If* I was right, if, *if.*

Accordingly, after a terrific lunch at the Frankfurterhof, we made the switch, packing up the merchandise in a nice quiet wood with the birds tweeting away up there in the summery trees, and we transferred the dodgy wheel from the three-point-four to the XK. The three hundred and sixty thousand marks I had in my pants pockets made it awfully difficult bending over to help the Archbubble with the wheel.

16

MARCHMARE and I sat in the airport restaurant, at the best table by the window where you could see out and watch the planes. Marchmare was dissecting a little smoked salmon between gulps of some very good hock. We were still congratulating each other over Reisemann—a very tough subject indeed, rendered, as they say in bomb-disposal circles, harmless.

'After a *most* unpromising beginning,' said Marchmare, flicking a bread pellet at me.

Looking at him, it was hard to believe last night had ever happened—the same old Marchmare, imperishable in the beautiful suit, the Fath tie, as cool as if he were in the Cavalryman to pay off a few slag for steering punters into the Archbubble's chemmy game, or calmly telling my father that wasn't a Jordaens at all, he'd been had . . . the very fair hair and the blue minces limpid as a deb's at her first kosher dance—till they suddenly went that agate colour on you.

I enjoyed that lunch. It's exciting, lunching expensively at airports with planes coming and going beyond the panoramic plate-glass windows and severe birds' voices butting in to order Herr Rosensohn to go to the Customs hall as if he were a dodgy punter trying to leave the game without paying. It gives you that international feeling.

And if there's something not too terrible ahead, like maybe taking a huge bundle of Deutschmarks to Switzerland all of your very own, it gives it just that little extra dash of sauce, doesn't it?

Marchmare was talking about wristwatches.

'Eighteen carat of course, morrie,' he said, signalling the waiter for another bottle of hock. 'I know they're cheaper in Belgium but you get a better choice in Geneva.'

'Patek-Philippe!' I breathed.

'Audemar-Piquet.'

'Omega Skymasters!'

'Oyster Perpetuals!'

'Patek are best.'

'No, Audemar.'

'Oh, well, if you go for that paper-thin kind.'

'Remember that awful vulgar one Bulbul had with the sapphire numerals? Cost him three ton.'

'He knocked, though.'

It was all in front of us. We were young. Suddenly we were rich. Say what you like, we had worked hard.

The metallic voice of the announcerette interrupted these deliberations.

'Flight 201 for Geneva, please,' it said. 'Proceed to Gate D all passengers for Geneva, please.'

'I must get some magazines to read on the plane,' said Marchmare.

'You can play rummy with me. Fifty quid a corner,' I said crossly.

'Oh, that's nursery stuff.'

'No, it isn't. Not if you play with a wild card.'

'I'll have them all, don't worry.'

'Ten-card Hollywood. It'll be a change from poker.'

'Fifty quid, that's six hundred marks.'

We strolled towards Gate D. 'I wish Christice were here, the old loyal,' I said, looking up out of the window at the lovely sky.

'She'd have hated it,' said Marchmare.

'Not this bit, she wouldn't.'

There was our plane, a streak of silver in the afternoon sun.

I thought back to the last plane I had taken, that night with Christice going to Paris. We climbed in with the drab old krauts and secured a window seat for Marchmare by murmuring 'Press, Press' in a grave and important way. Then we got the broads out.

'Your deal, morrie.'

'Straight or bent?'

The motors revved to their sharp, harsh limit and the plane shuddered a little under the brakes. Then it taxied and raced down the runway, swerving a little, like a wounded bird. I felt the bump as we came off and we were up, away into the blue. I wasn't really paying attention and Marchmare won the first round of rummy. I didn't play again at once. I looked out of the window thinking: Hell, it'll probably be all right, and thinking some of those funny things you can never quite think. I even thought: With that loot in the bank I wouldn't mind a kosher little farmhouse in West Sussex somewhere and perhaps marry Christice to see what happened. After all, you had to marry someone in the death, everyone did.

'We won't take up Reisemann's proposition,' I said aloud.

'Hell,' said Marchmare, 'I would. Any day, rather than land in the nick.'

His head was bent, he was shuffling the cards. Suddenly I thought: None of this would be any fun if it weren't for him. He had a kind of genius that made him the epitaph on the tombstone of 1962—that tremendous impulse to money and power and heartlessness and living well and pushing a lucky streak as far as it would go. I noticed him in that minute and thought: It's funny, it's as if I've never really seen him before. While I watched he deliberately took an old bit of chewing-gum out of his mouth and deposited the lump carefully on the top of the seat behind so that the old kraut would be almost sure to get it in his hair next time he leaned back. You can't get it out, you know. He popped in a new bit and displayed it on the end of his tongue, smiling like an elderly baby. A lot of viscous white cloud swept by, reminding me of Christice's breasts.

'More cards, morrie,' said Marchmare indistinctly, behind his gum. 'Your deal.'

For practice I dealt us both an ace in a hand of five-card stud. In an hour, the hostess was saying to someone behind us, we would be there.

At Geneva Airport we went out into the sun and took a taxi. Marchmare, who had walked slowly out of the building, seemed nervous, hunching himself up in the cab to lean forward and peer into the driver's mirror.

'What's the matter with you, morrie?' I said after a while, as we sped off towards the banking centre in the middle of the city.

'Speak Spanish,' he said seriously in that language. 'I don't trust Swiss taxi-drivers any more than German ones.'

I stared at him in astonishment.

'Go on,' he said, 'be a big fat business man from Barcelona.'

So we started speaking Spanish.

'We're being followed, don't you see?' he said presently.

I looked backwards, but for the life of me I couldn't see any signs of it.

'Not now,' said Marchmare, 'back at the airport.'

'Who was it?'

'You didn't spot them?' said Marchmare astonished. 'Three.' He said in English: 'With the newspapers. Law written all over them.'

I had never heard him say 'newspapers' before.

We reached the city centre. Marchmare leaned forward and tapped the driver on the shoulder. I followed him out on to the pavement. 'But we don't know where we are,' I said. I wasn't familiar with Geneva.

'There's the Crédit Suisse,' he said impatiently, jerking his head. I looked up the high grey street. I could see several other banks.

We started walking towards them. They were on the opposite side of the street to us. 'Don't hurry,' said Marchmare. We stopped and looked into a window. Ironically, it was full of watches. Presently a man with a newspaper under his arm walked purposefully past us and joined the crowd crossing the street at the lights fifty yards further up.

'They didn't bother to follow our car,' said Marchmare, 'did you notice? It's because they already guessed where we were going.'

'Why don't they arrest us here, then?' I said.

'I think because they want to wait and see what we're going to do. They've obviously sussed we're only here for a bit of banking, and they can't decide whether to pinch us and the loot now or hang around and hope we lead them back to krautland and Reisemann.'

'And then back to the U.K. with the slush.'

'Exactly,' said Marchmare. 'So they'd rather keep the obbs on us here than get a warrant.'

'Do you think it's Swiss law?' I said.

'Some of it—but some of it must be Interpol. *Hell*,' said, Marchmare, staring into the window and using it as a mirror, 'I can't see the other two.'

I thought it over and made a plan. 'Well, at least,' I said, 'they won't stop us banking this lot.'

I told him my plan.

'Hell,' he said, 'it's splendid, morrie. Won't they be choked?' Still, there it was. The law.

'Come on,' said Marchmare, 'let's get moving. Towards all those banks.' There were three in a row. 'The law'll wait for us to catch up with it.'

'By the way,' I said, 'you realize we've got to go back to Germany.'

'Oh, to hell with Germany,' he said.

'I'm sorry,' I said. 'Like you once said, both our skins hang on this deal. This time you'll do as I say. We ought to have long ago.'

He was angry. 'Why have we got to go back to dreary krautland? Hell, darling, it's a frightful drag.'

'To pick up the motor, of course,' I said.

He whistled. 'I'd forgotten.'

'I hadn't.'

'Well, we'll just have to leave it.'

I thought for only a second. 'We can't,' I said. 'That's not nearly good enough.'

He said something unprintable. '*Why* not?'

'For the simple reason it's all over Mike's dabs from London. That'd be all they'd need, wouldn't it? It'll have to be wiped— better still, burned.'

He was all about trout now. 'If they haven't already found it.'

'They won't have,' I said. 'Not yet.'

But we were in a big jam.

'How'd they get on to us so quick?' I marvelled, not needing an answer.

'They took Mike at his word,' said Marchmare slowly. 'Christ help him.'

And his eyes were that agate, like a snake's.

I was glad I wasn't in Mike's shoes.

We walked slowly on up the street. It was a funny feeling, knowing Old Bill was after us. I hadn't got used to it yet. One minute the world had been smiling for us; now the sun had set on us in the afternoon. The money in my pockets felt like lead.

'Get ready,' I said. I wanted to wet my pants. Also I wanted to go up to the little man who had walked purposefully past us with law written all over him and smash his face in till it was just a blob. But I forced myself to be calm. It nearly killed me.

'O.K.,' said Marchmare. 'Let's have it quick, darling.'

'Well, the main thing being to cover our tracks,' I said, watching the busy street. 'Right now there's nothing but pure sus. If they can't match it up with some proof somehow they've had it. Thank Christ we passed the merchandise to the bubble.'

'I know,' said Marchmare impatiently. 'So?'

Just then a big black jam drew up outside the Crédit Suisse and I saw the man who had passed us stoop to talk to the occupants. They weren't taking any trouble about hiding themselves. I wanted to top the lot of them. Then the thing I was waiting for appeared at last, screeching slowly round the corner. 'O.K.,' I said to Marchmare, 'here's your big moment. Get on that tram. Get back to the airport and book on the first plane. Then slip into the loo. Change your face. Comb your hair the other side. Wear dark glasses if you have to, but don't forget the linens have lots of pictures of you wearing those. Just don't look obvious. Fade into the scene. Get to Frankfurt and wipe that motor. Or anything. I don't care what you do with it as long as it disappears. Ditch it if you must. Set it alight if you can. It's about the most wanted motor in Europe.'

'And you?'

'I'll bank the loot and take care of the law,' I said. 'They'll get in the hell of a flap when they find we've split up. *They* don't know which twin has the Toni.' I watched the tram. 'O.K. for money?'

'Yeeh.'

'Passport?'

'Sure.'

'Then get back to the U.K. like all hell get out and wait for old cocked hat and whiskers to knock. Believe me, he won't be long.'

The tram ground to a halt and Marchmare dropped into the queue that shambled up to it.

'No exhibitionism now,' I said severely.

'Good luck, morrie.'

'Good luck.'

The tram started with a jerk, bell clanging dolefully, and watching that police jam I saw a certain amount of disorder and haste on the pavement. Two of the law plunged into the jam; as the third opened the door for them I slipped across the street against the lights, dodging the traffic, and then ran like the hammers up the street past the Crédit Suisse to the Geneva Kreditbank. I pushed through the swing doors and saw that the main hall was full. Looking away from the commissionaire I went up to the nearest grille, forcing myself not to hurry. I merged gratefully into the people waiting and made myself look at nothing and think about nothing, the best way I know of looking like nothing much.

'I want to see the manager,' I said when it was my turn and still speaking in Spanish. 'I want a numbered account.' The clerk paused and I looked nervously around. It would never do to stay in this hall a second longer than necessary.

'The door over there,' said the clerk at last, without looking up from his computor. 'Room thirty. Second floor.'

It was like the tape-recorders all over again except that the angst was, if possible, even more pressing. However, I sauntered over to the corner of the hall he had indicated and pushed open a door leading to a staircase. On it a notice said: 'Generaldirektion. Zimmer 30.' Now I could run at last, and I took the stairs two and three at a time. The second floor was a long passage with two girls hurrying down it in the distance. It offered less cover than a billiard table. I found Room 30 and walked in as slowly as I could. A fat, pale man in a light-blue suit was sitting at a massive desk smoking a cigar and dictating to a secretary. He looked up at my unheralded appearance in some surprise and annoyance. A board on the desk displayed the name 'H. H. Wurter'.

'I'm English,' I said, 'and I'm in a big hurry. I've got some very important business to do with you.'

'I've got some letters to finish,' he said crossly.

'I can't help that,' I said flatly. 'I've got a plane to catch.'

I pulled the money out and piled it on his desk. 'Three hundred and sixty thousand marks,' I said. 'A numbered account.'

His expression changed. He dismissed the secretary with a nod. She went out looking haughty and ruffled.

Wurter was smiling. 'How do I know you haven't robbed a bank?' he was saying, as he counted the money with a fat finger and chuckling.

'What?' I said, as if amazed. 'Me?'

'You Englishmen,' said Herr Wurter. 'You are all the same.

Wherever you are you behave as if you were at home and your word was law.'

I had been prepared to make it law if there'd been any difficulty, believe me, but there wasn't, though Herr Wurter was one of the most maddeningly slow people I have ever seen. There were endless formalities, in the middle of which he pushed over a large box of cigars. I took one with a certain detached interest to see if I could smoke it. I did, but it nearly choked me. In my hurry I had forgotten about all the papers that had to be filled in. I produced my bent passport and he stared for a long moment from the photograph to me. I was ready for anything then.

'A good likeness,' he said at last, wreathed in smiles. He locked the money in his safe and returned the passport. I forced myself to approach all these obstacles at a normal speed, only twice allowing myself to look at my watch and express anxiety at the passage of time. But Herr Wurter, it seemed, had masses of time. Finally, though, it was finished; and I had just given Herr Wurter a specimen signature of the phoney Mr. Johnson in my passport when the expected interruption occurred.

Herr Wurter's secretary put her head round the door. 'Excuse me,' she said. 'There are two Herren wishing to see the *auslander* Herr.'

It made me furious. It was so obvious they hadn't got a warrant yet: if they had they could have arrested us any time. No. As it was, they were hoping to frighten me into telling them where Marchmare was. He had plainly given them the slip. It was the law trying to pull a stroke and I thought: Right, you've messed me about enough for one day. Now it's my turn.

'Ah,' I said to Wurter, in what I hoped was a voice of surprise and pleasure, 'my friends. They've arrived earlier than I expected.' To his secretary I said: 'Please ask them to wait.'

'Why don't you have them in?' beamed Herr Wurter. 'Our private business is all finished now.'

'I think I won't,' I said, 'if you don't mind.'

We both rose from our chairs and it occurred to me how the law must be boiling with rage. How they'd have loved to relieve me of all that loot. Now they were too late. That was the wonderful thing about Swiss banks if you had a numbered account; once they'd agreed to bank it you were just a code number. Kosher-looking Englishmen never had much difficulty in Geneva. And when the bank was satisfied, any questions, from Interpol upwards and downwards, simply went unanswered, and no matter what happened that little sum would always be sitting there waiting for us. Another point: even now the law couldn't know that we hadn't played it even cooler: even now they weren't *sure* if my act in the bank wasn't maybe a blind. For all they knew Marchmare could be happily batting on to the next town and be banking the loot there. But of course the law would be alerted everywhere. The place was simply crawling with law. An Interpol job. I didn't like it at all. And continental police didn't bother about appearances much, as I knew from Spain. If they didn't get what they wanted on the hurry-up they didn't hesitate to . . .

'I'd be glad, Herr Wurter,' I said as we parted amid fulsome goodbyes, 'to know that my affairs are held in complete secrecy.'

'But of course they are,' he said, genuinely shocked.

To make quite sure, I memorized the code number and letters Wurter had written out for me, and as I walked through the secretary's office I slipped the paper into my mouth and swallowed it. Now I mustn't forget the number—but I have a memory like a lynx for numbers like that.

As I opened the door into the passage I knew how I was going to deal with the law. I opened it sharply and purposefully, walked fast through it. As I'd expected I nearly hit one of them in the chest. He grunted, but automatically stepped aside. I started walking quickly down that long corridor without looking back. A second later I heard the patter of tiny booted feet and found a well-fed figure on either side of me. I didn't let the grass grow.

'Well?' I snapped, still walking, 'who the hell are you? What do you want? I haven't much time.'

'We know that,' said the one on my left softly. He flapped a wallet under my nose. 'Police.'

'What police?' I jeered. 'Keystone Cops?'

'You vill not make yourself much deals with that talk,' said the person, put out. So I'd learned one thing about him. If you were nasty to him his English went off the boil. It was a start.

'Geneva police,' said the one on my right, dimly.

'I don't care,' I said, 'what sort of police you are.' I was walking very fast all the time and the one on my right practically had to canter to keep up with me. 'I'm in a hell of a hurry. Where are we going?'

'To police headquarters for a little talk,' said the one on my left, who seemed to be senior.

'Okay,' I said, 'what's the charge?' We were at the head of the stairs.

He pretended to sound surprised. 'Charge?' He tried to look no end cunning and dodgy. 'Ah, then, so you are afeared.'

'I'm afeared of missing my plane,' I said, 'that's all. And you've got to have a charge. Especially for foreigners travelling abroad. Got a warrant?'

'Warrant?' said the senior one in a voice that was meant to sound slow and sinister. 'Ve haf no warrant.'

I stopped my cracking pace halfway downstairs and turned to look at him. 'Well, then,' I said, 'you're wasting your time, aren't you?' I forced myself to keep on looking choked. 'Hell,' I said. 'What do you think this is? Afternoon off for the dumb chums' society?'

I watched their peeved-looking boats. This wasn't the kind of reception they'd bargained for. It was me who'd been supposed to get the reception, anyway.

But, after Reisemann, what were two dumb-looking Swiss cops?

'All we want,' said the senior, 'is a little talk with you for just fifteen minutes in the *recherche* room at the station.'

I didn't fancy the sound of the *recherche* room at all. 'I'm afraid it's out of the question,' I said, looking at my watch.

By this time we were at street level.

'See?' said the senior one, pointing and attempting a bit of jollity that sounded sadly forced, 'we haf even a car to take you in. No need to walk!' And there was that big black motor, with the third member of the party, whose job seemed to be holding open the door, duly holding open the door and earning his keep. The one who had followed us was sitting in the back, eating a large sandwich.

'Poor sergeant,' said the senior sadly to me, 'he was much delayed following you. See? He has not yet had even his lunch.'

I remarked that this was a great pity, suppressing a strong temptation to giggle.

'Ve haf your friend belonging,' said the other one sullenly. The senior one regarded him with an expression that looked like irritation. It *was* rather a stupid approach.

'What friend?' I said.

'The Herr we saw you at the airport with descend.'

But I had had all that cobblers while they were still saving up to go to police night school.

'I've no idea what you're talking about,' I said, 'unless you mean the tiresome, talkative young person I gave a lift to.'

They were silent for a minute. Finally the senior one said: 'Your passport please, mein Herr.'

I played this minor trump. They turned it over and over, scanning the photograph and comparing it to one they evidently had.

'Well?' I said. 'Now what?'

They didn't seem to know. Then the senior one pronounced pompously: 'Ve think she is forged, yes.'

I exploded with laughter. 'Good God!' I said. 'Would you mind telling me just who you think I am?'

'Ve think you are this person who must to the polizeiamt be belonging.'

'Okay,' I said, 'prove it. But, I warn you, if you're wrong I've got an uncle in the Foreign Office who'll have both your necks wrung like a couple of chickens.'

And, believe it or not, the first part of this statement was true.

They wavered even more. No copper likes that sort of threat unless he knows exactly where he is, and these didn't. I could almost see them thinking: Hell, this isn't even our pigeon. It's an Interpol job.

I jumped in at once. 'Now listen,' I continued. 'Face facts. You're making a mistake. You've no warrant, no charge and the name on your papers isn't the name on this passport. So look, Superintendent,' I said more kindly, 'let's call it a day, shall we? I don't know what my firm will say if I miss this plane.'

The younger one seized eagerly on this. 'What is the name of this firm?' he said.

'As-You-Like-It-Investments Limited,' I answered firmly, making a mental note to appoint Mr. Johnson to the board as soon as I got home. 'Rome Street, London.'

They were horribly torn. I could see their orderly Swiss minds outraged by the strange turns this apparently routine matter had taken.

The senior one played his last card. 'Ve can in three hours an English police who positively can identify you.'

Plinth, I thought. 'Well,' I said, 'it's up to you. If you want to hold me I certainly can't stop you.' I looked him straight in the face and spoke my next words very slowly. 'But I can tell you here and now, that if you wrongfully arrest me it'll be your neck and your colleague's. I shall,' I said, 'be merciless.'

He gave up. 'I cannot force you,' he said grudgingly, 'I haf not the evidence belonging.'

'I think you're being very sensible,' I said gravely, allowing myself a slight smile and no more. I held out my hand. 'We'll forget it, shall we?'

He took it as briefly as possible. Dislike seemed to be mutual.

Perhaps it wasn't surprising. 'I still do not understand the photograph,' he said, 'which seems the same.'

'Oh, hell,' I said, whistling for a cab, 'you know what passport photos are like. They all look the same. Terrible.' A cab slid up and I opened the door.

' 'Bye-bye then,' I said, getting in. They peered in at me mournfully. The cab moved off and I had a last glimpse of the junior law scuffing the pavement irritably with the toe of his shoe.

I leaned forward to the driver. '*Fahren*,' I said. '*Nach Lufthaven. Aber schnell.*'

Geneva was about the hottest city on earth for yours truly at that moment, and deviators who tell you oh the quaint old continental law shouldn't. It's all cobblers.

17

THE cab stopped at the main airport building. I'd been unwise to take one like that under the law's nose, but what else could I do? It was six o'clock as I hurried through the crowds speculating on how soon I could get a plane.

Making myself inconspicuous and hugging the walls, I dived over to the information desk and asked the blonde, naughty-looking bird what time the next plane left for Paris. In Paris I could go to ground with a deviator I know in Rue Jacob, get my breath back and generally assess the angst.

'In half an hour,' she said, but added with a phlegmatic Swiss shrug, 'but you will not get on it. It is full.'

'Okay,' I said impatiently. 'Big deal. So what time's the next one?'

She surveyed me with bovine contempt. 'At 2015,' she replied. 'But what does it matter? They are all full. Only the midnight plane may have seats.'

This was far too late.

'Rome, then?' I hazarded. 'Or Madrid?'

'Nothing till 2230.'

Of course, it was midsummer, and the uprush of slags and squares had burst on Europe like a boil. It was hopeless and I left her, stalking furiously towards the bar. If there was one thing I needed now it was a drink—but very quick, while I thought up the next move. For in spite of my high-handed attitude with Old Bill I had only a respite, half an hour at the outside. In a place like this they would be up with me again in no time; they would of course have taken the number of the cab I'd used . . . and here I was futilely strolling about in the most obvious spot in the city.

I walked into the airport bar and saw Marchmare immediately. He spotted me the same second; he looked rather pale and was drumming his fingers nervously on the counter. But he slipped off his stool smoothly and followed me out.

'What the hell are you doing here?' I muttered as we walked about with our heads bent.

'No plane.'

'What did you do about that motor?'

'The only thing I could think of,' he said. 'I sent Reisemann a telegram telling him to destroy it any way he could.'

'Oh, you *fool*, morrie,' I whispered savagely. 'They'll track that.'

'I couldn't help it. It was that or have them catch it.'

'Maybe they'll do both,' I said gloomily. But I was glad to see him. Angst is halved when shared.

'How did you get on at the bank?' he asked.

I told him. He screamed with laughter. '*Goodness*, how loyal!'

I admired him at that moment. Angst all round us thick as the arrows at noonday, and there he was hooting with laughter.

We were walking towards the exit as we spoke, and just as we reached it I saw something that made me snatch Marchmare and drag him behind a row of automatic machines. It was that fat old motor again and all our friends were in it. We ran back into the shelter of the airport hall. It was doubtful shelter. The dim, hopeless crowds drifting about in holiday hats could conceal stacks of law.

Suddenly Marchmare altered direction. 'Look,' he murmured, nodding to a sign. 'Car park. Steal a motor?' he whispered, and God help me his boat was glistening with excitement.

I thought quickly.

'What about the train?' I said.

'Hopeless,' he said. 'Far too slow and obvious. They'd get us before it crossed the frontier. No,' he went on, as we sidled up to the swing-doors through which we could see the car park, 'stealing a motor's the only hope.'

'How far'll we take it?' I said.

'As far as we can,' he said grimly.

'What about when we get to the frontier?'

'I know where we can crash that into Germany. On the Zürich-Munich road. I did it before once when I was working for Bulbul. There's no gate.'

'Right,' I said. 'Let's go.'

'Do you see any law you recognize?'

I looked about. 'No.'

'Well,' said Marchmare, 'we'll just have to make a quick dive for it.'

We did, pelting across the wide road, into the trees the other side and over the fence into the car park. We were only just in time. Looking back at the building I saw a man in an overcoat walk up and lean against the wall by the door we'd just left.

'And what's more,' said Marchmare gleefully, 'he's got a shooter. Just *look* at his pocket, poor old darling. And fancy an overcoat in this weather! And *so* dragged out of shape. Must be a howitzer at least.'

We joined unobtrusively on to the tail of a group of airport-workers who were coming off shift and making for their cars. We looked about us.

'There!' said Marchmare, nudging me and pointing. 'That's what we want.'

It was a big black Mercedes 220S, spanking new and standing by itself in a corner of the park quite close to us, looking smug and grand. We went over to it casually, made certain there was no one about and then squatted down behind it. I read off its registration plate without thinking and came to with a jerk when I saw the letters C.D. at the end.

'Look,' I said to Marchmare. '*Corps Diplomatique*, see? That'll make the frontiers a bit easier.'

'Okay,' he whispered. 'Will you fix the starter, morrie?'

'I will if I can get in,' I muttered.

'Oh, we'll get in all right,' said Marchmare. He was more confident than I was. We'd got nothing to bust the lock with. But he was right. Cautiously, he felt upwards towards the handle of the driver's door and it gave. Probably the chauffeur was just having his smoke break over at the airport café.

'Quick, then,' I said to Marchmare. 'Inside. The bonnet. It opens from inside.' The jam was identical to the one I used while I was conning an old boiler in New York in '59. 'It's the last knob to the right under the dash.'

He had it in a moment with that serpentine agility of his, and I heard the 'bump' as the bonnet disengaged from the radiator grille. In an instant my hand had freed the safety catch and was groping in the engine for the red and green wires from the distributor to the ignition switch, blessing the day when Dodge O'Toole up on Warren Street had taught me, in an idle moment, how to start a motor on the hurry-up with no key. 'When I give the word,' I said, 'poke the starter and we're away. Anyone coming?'

'No,' he said. 'But be quick, morrie.'

'I am being,' I said irritably, as I tore out the two wires I wanted. 'Okay,' I said, connecting the bare ends. 'Start her.'

He did. I got a mild shock and swore. The motor whirred, died. He tried again. It was perceptibly weaker this time—Christ, the battery was going to be flat down to the chauffeur . . . from Toade I knew all about them and their well-it's-not-my-motor attitude. 'Choke!' I shouted. 'It's automatic! Put your foot down as far as you can and try again.'

'Okay!' said Marchmare's voice faintly. The motor whirred again and fired. Marchmare slipped in the automatic drive as I slammed down the bonnet and the car was on the move as I got in. We circled the huge park. Distantly, the plane we had failed to catch drifted down the runway and hit the air, its lights winking slowly in the twilight. As we nosed out into the road I looked back, but there seemed to be no activity from the law.

Marchmare swerved suddenly. 'For Christ's sake!' I shouted. 'This is no time for an accident.' The petrol truck he had just missed bumped back into the road off the pavement, the driver screaming and going ahead. '*Do* try and drive sensibly, darling,' I begged. Marchmare's exhibitionism could still ruin us.

By the time we reached the city limits I was sure we weren't being followed. I found a homburg on the back seat and popped it on my head. It was miles too big. I put it on Marchmare's. It fitted.

'Your head was always bigger than mine,' I said.

Soon we were on the main Munich road. Marchmare put his foot down and the jam shot forward. We drove on very fast, I guiding him from a big-scale touring map which I found in the passenger's pocket. There were also maps of Austria and Germany which showed up yet another piece of territory I wanted to know all about, which belonged to neither country. Better still, I found a current carnet in the car. True, it was useless for inspection, but it was handy to have to wave as we beetled past startled guards. It was growing dark. In three hours —or less, at this rate—we'd be out of Switzerland. The traffic was light. With any luck, if the morrie gods were kind, which they had been, considering the angst, the car wouldn't be traced till we were far into Germany.

We took care at the speed limits. The last thing we could afford was a john from a traffic cop. Suddenly it all began to seem very funny. We bent double as howls of laughter swept us.

18

I T HAD to be Reisemann, via Czechoslovakia. If you looked at the situation rationally, there was nothing else left.

When I told Marchmare the car described a crazy swoop across the road.

'Me too,' he said, yawning languidly. 'I shall do it for the *frisson*.'

It was the least pressing and most agreeable reason for doing it.

'Of course, we're mad, morrie,' said Marchmare.

'Not I,' I said hastily. 'I'm as sane as anything.'

'But London, morrie,' said Marchmare, pained. 'The bird. Winston's.'

'It'll have to take its course without us for a while,' I said primly. 'If you came to think of it, it would anyhow, if Old Bill got hold of us. Slow up. You turn left here.'

'Now *that's* very true, morrie,' said Marchmare, making his turn and doing ninety up the left-hand side of the road, which was narrow.

'They drive on the right here, I believe,' I croaked, as casually as I could.

It was hard not to laugh. Everything had got out of hand so fast, like a motor accident. It was difficult to realize that we had still been on the right side of Old Bill this time twenty-four hours ago. Now we were wanted everywhere and were hurtling across Switzerland in a stolen jamjar. At least we had plenty of money. I think I always knew it would happen. Like when you know you're going to win or lose at a game of no-peeky baseball. I looked out of the window a minute at the villages dwarfed by the mountains, at the road zooming past. Switzerland, outpost of the West . . . gas station . . . *Bibliotek* . . . *Gaststatter*. Zipping by. It was too much. I leaned under the dash and switched on the radio. We picked up A.F.N.

'Super pop,' said Marchmare.

We had stopped a while back for petrol and bought some brandy. Now I produced this and we drank the raw spirit in gulps and listened to the cool beat of American jazz, symbol of everything we were leaving.

Marchmare echoed my thoughts some way further on. 'Seems dead strange to be making the trip from West to East, doesn't it, when most ice-creams are bursting to do it the other way, morrie.'

But most of the time we stayed stumm. Marchmare was giving the car everything it could take on the winding passes and I'll say this for him: he kept it on the road. It grew dark, and in the beam of the headlights jagged forests rose steeply on either side of us. Luckily it was summer—at least we hadn't any snowfalls to reckon with. At about nine it began to rain, though, which added to Marchmare's problems. But by this time we were only eighty kilometres from Zürich and another two hours would see us at Rorschach and the kraut frontier. Personally, I hoped the rain would keep up. Frontier guards tend to stick in their shelters. I got our passports and insurance card ready just in case.

If anyone had set up a road-block this side of Germany, I thought, it was going to be just too bad for somebody.

It happened just beyond the Zürichsee, a scant forty miles from the frontier, where the road crawls upwards to the mountains that separate Germany from Switzerland. We were cursing and screaming because we had got behind a stream of heavy traffic making its placid Swiss way uphill at about twenty, which was about a quarter of the speed we wanted to go. Then all at once it slowed even more. Then the heavy truck in front of us stopped with a grunt of air brakes.

'For Christ's sake,' I said, 'lean out and see what's going on.'

'It's lights,' said Marchmare. 'They're flashing torches in the road. They're stopping everyone.'

It was pointless musing on it—it was a police check, whether for our benefit or not was arguable and academic. I opened my mouth to speak, but Marchmare had already acted. The Mercedes swept far out on to the left of the road, which was Marchmare's favourite side anyhow, and with lights blazing tore up the road at full power alongside the assorted lorries. If there had been time I should have felt sick, because it took the law just that second to clock what was happening, and it might have been his last but one. He was all alone. I could see his motor-cycle parked by the kerb. Marchmare approached him doing 120 km. and somehow he jumped, a wild flying figure in the headlights, and made it on to the bonnet of the truck whose driver he'd been talking to. But we couldn't avoid his bike, though in fact we only grazed it and sent it belting into the wall. A pair of headlights appeared straight in our path coming downhill, but we missed them with a foot to spare, got back on the right-hand side of the road and we were through.

After this the frontier was easy. We reached it in twenty-five minutes. A green-clad figure sauntered amiably out of a sentry-box to chat and say hello, but we nearly had his toes off and were through Lustenau and into Germany before you could say ´ski-instructor' backwards.

Ten minutes inside Germany we changed over. I switched on the interior light and saw Marchmare's face as he climbed into the passenger's seat. It was chalk white and sweaty.

A minute after we started again delayed shock hit me too in the form of shivering fits which shook me so that I could hardly keep the motor on the road.

I bypassed Kempten, of course; it was too big—and hit a small road to the south-east near Garmisch; this took us in a long slant towards the Austrian frontier. It was getting late and the little Niederbayern villages were all asleep. The peacefulness helped us relax. We lowered the windows so that the warm night air filled the car; all round us was silence broken by the rush of our tyres on the cobbles, crickets chirping in the invisible fields and the low mutter of the radio which Marchmare constantly moved from station to station in search of a news bulletin. We suddenly realized how tired we were. We had driven three hundred and twenty miles in seven hours, which was nothing short of fantastic on those roads. We had made three stops for petrol and had wanted to eat, but knew we mustn't. Passau and the Czech frontier at Plocklstein were still a hundred and thirty miles away.

Garmisch, Partenkirchen, Oberammergau . . . it was a sad business leaving them behind. My mind slipped back three years to a winter holiday with a bird; we bought a car in Stuttgart and drove it to Innsbruck; we saw the New Year in just over the Italian frontier at Pieve di Cadore and drove on to Venice, where we stood hand in hand in the deserted Piazza and were overwhelmed by the bells of the campanile which struck in antiquity through the deep fog coming in from the sea. We knew passion in Salzburg, rest in Mittelwald, the money ran out in Linz, but we recouped in Seefeld, playing poker in the Salzburgerhof with three half-cut Americans in ski-boots.

'Listen!' said Marchmare suddenly. A B.B.C. news bulletin filtered through.

'The police are anxious to contact three young men whom they think can help them in their inquiries regarding alleged breaches of the Exchange Control Act. Two of them were seen this afternoon in Geneva, Switzerland. The third is believed to be in Antwerp. Anyone having information about them is requested to contact New Scotland Yard. . . .'

'Well,' I said, 'now we know.'

'*Goodness*, how loyal!' said Marchmare. 'Exchange Control Act, indeed! Wait till everyone *really* hears.'

'They soon will,' I said. 'Don't worry. About tomorrow or the day after. Every linen in Europe will carry it.'

'And then gracious what a flap there'll be,' said Marchmare. We were passing through a tiny village and he lit a fireball which he tossed gaily out of the window. 'And of course we'll sell our story to the linens somehow, and make a right few quid out of that.'

'I wouldn't be too sure,' I said.

'Oh, shup.'

'Shup shelf.'

'I wonder how the Archbubble got on?' I said.

'No need to worry about him. Those crafty old bubbles always make it okay.'

But an hour later we heard on an A.F.N. broadcast that he'd been picked up trying to embark at Hamburg. The announcer made no reference to it, but of course they'd have found the merchandise.

Marchmare took the wheel again while we were south of Muehldorf. It was 3 a.m. and we reckoned to make the Czech frontier by a quarter to five.

'God I'm tired.'

'So'm I,' I said, yawning.

'Don't you think we could stop and kip in the motor for a bit?'

'I don't think it'd be at all wise, morrie.'

'It's rather splendid there hasn't been any more angst from the law, isn't it?'

'I don't think it ever supposed we'd be heading east,' I said.

'What are we going to actually do when we get to the frontier?' said Marchmare.

I too had been pondering this for quite a while. There was only one answer really, but one hated to admit it.

'I mean,' he said, 'you know what those sort of people are like.'

'They couldn't be tougher than Reisemann.'

'As a matter of fact,' said Marchmare, 'I think they could. Not so educated, you know.'

'Well,' I said, 'there's no point in dwelling on that part of it.'

'You're sure you want to go, morrie? I mean, *I'm* going, but I could easily drop you off.'

'Good God,' I said, 'of course I want to go. Think of the alternative.'

We spent a minute or so thinking of the alternative.

'We seem to have done everything a bit too brown this time, morrie.'

'Well, never mind,' I said, 'I suppose it had to happen.'

'Think of all that bird where we're going,' said Marchmare. 'We'll teach it to rock. It's so *square*. Revolutionary bird always is.'

'And we'll show it how to go bohemian.'

Somehow, though, it was difficult to work up any wild enthusiasm about our destination. At this distance even the slag in the King's Road seemed preferable.

I remembered meeting several of their students at a United Nations reception in New York. They wore suits made, apparently, of papier maché which cracked when they put their soft drinks down. They were crop-headed and as exciting to talk to as the I-speak-your-weight machine at Waterloo. Still, I didn't want to depress him too much.

'We'll settle down in no time,' I said. 'You see if we don't.'

'Yes,' said Marchmare, 'no doubt, dearie. Well now, about this crossing-the-frontier lark—perhaps we could moody them into letting us through. We could get them to put a call to Reisemann at Kassburg.'

'Are you *mad*?' I said. 'He won't be there. Kassburg was only a one-night stand. Besides, there won't be any time for moody, if you come to think of it—you don't suppose the krauts aren't going to *notice* this motor, do you?' In the cold light of dawn our new escapade looked very thin. I felt the let-down of fatigue, alone and uncared for in a hard, cold world.

'Oh, don't *put* difficulties in the way, morrie!' screamed Marchmare. 'Really, you are so *depressing* sometimes.'

'I was just trying to work it all out,' I said, 'that's all.'

'Sometimes I think you've got no guts.'

'Well,' I said, 'perhaps I haven't.' It was something I was never sure of.

We were very much on edge.

'Anyway,' said Marchmare in a voice a note too high, 'I'm *not* going to jail, dearie. That's one thing I promise you.' He was silent for a moment. 'I'd go potty in there.' He braked the car viciously on a corner and we streamed uphill towards the sky, which was turning a dirty yellow colour.

'Of course not,' I said. 'Besides, it'd be so annoying sitting there thinking about how nasty Plinth and the law had won.'

'Exactly, morrie. It would never do.'

I drew a deep breath. 'It'll have to be another Rorschach job then, won't it?' I said. Frankly, I didn't care for the idea at all. Not with the Czechs. But it was that or turn back and do bird.

'Yes,' said Marchmare, 'that's right.'

'Let me drive, then,' I said.

'No, no, morrie. I'll do it.'

'Hell,' I said, 'it's my turn to crash a frontier. You've done one.'

'That was an easy one with no gate. I want to do one with a gate *and* lots of guards with shooters. I'm going to do it, anyway. When we get to it just get down on the floor and make yourself small.'

'There'll be two posts, don't forget,' I said. 'The krauts and then them.'

'I know.'

'You're sure you'll do it?'

'Quite sure,' he said, 'dearie.'

Then we sat in silence, watching the scenery whirring past

us in the improving light. I was lighting us both a cigarette when he turned to me and said: 'Sorry if I got cross, morrie.'

'That's all right,' I said.

'Bit on edge, I suppose.'

It was all very kosher and British.

'Not surprising,' I said. 'It's been an angstful sort of night.'

19

I HAD been looking at the petrol needle, which was registering nearly empty again; then I think I must have sloped off into a doze, for the next thing I remember was Marchmare shaking me. I came to with a start. It was bitterly cold at the altitude we had reached and I shivered. The dawn was quite clear in the sky. The whole world seemed to have huddled up into itself. Everything was very still. I looked at my watch. It was twenty past five.

'I think we must be nearly there,' said Marchmare in a low voice. 'We came through Passau about five minutes ago. Look at the map.'

I picked it up off the floor and flattened it out. We were at the point where the German, Austrian and Czech frontiers converge. Looking up from the map I stared ahead. Far below us stretched a flat yellow plain; I thought I could even make out a murky glimmer which must be the Moldau. To the south and behind us was the obliterating mass of the Austrian Alps. 'This is it, then,' I mused, my forefinger on the map. Everything that had happened up to now seemed false and unreal. It was the difference between the long unsolved formula and ex equals nought. Living now meant the map, the stooping shape of Marchmare beside me and the whispering of the engine, the car we had brought twisting and shaking, cunning as a shark, across this huge tract of Europe all the way from Geneva.

'Well?' said Marchmare impatiently, biting his lip.

'Oh,' I said, 'I'm sorry . . . make for Plocklstein. It's about ten kilometres.'

We moved off up a bad road, climbing above massive forests, the endless mountains piling up into a white brilliant sky where a bird was singing. It was June the thirtieth, I thought, a date to remember, whatever happened. I saw everything hard and clear in a harsh economy of detail, taking in the final balance which had somehow turned out to be a debit one. My nerves were bad, though. Christ, I ought to be used to all this, I thought angrily. It's no worse than the tape-recorders. But it was. It was much worse than the Spanish frontier had been. They would be waiting for us this time, definitely. That was the bad bit, the definitely. And it wasn't like the fear that gripped you when you saw the other man had a gun. That was over in a second. Things happened quickly and humanely then; there wasn't time to be afraid. And action rescued you from fear, the absolute necessity for staying alive. So, partly, did your faith in chance. There was, as a matter of fact, only one chance, and this was it, and it looked very small indeed, lost in the odds. I wouldn't have backed it in front of the telly at the Tealeaf for anything.

We came to a bend in the road and there was the sign, black on white, which said: 'Halt. *Zoll.*' We crawled round it, and there was the Customs house.

Marchmare stopped.

'Okay, morrie,' he said, 'let's have that flask.'

We both had a swallow. Then Marchmare held it up. 'To the East!' he said, and we finished up all the brandy there was left. Then Marchmare hurled the flask out of the window.

He switched out the overdrive. 'I'll keep it in third,' he said seriously. 'Ready?'

I tensed myself.

'Ready,' I said.

He let the brake go and put his foot down flat on the floor. The car bucked like a frantic animal and the tyres yelled.

'Get down, morrie, get down!' he shouted. 'You'll be topped.'

But I kept my eyes just above the windscreen right up to the last second, staring in dreadful fascination as if it was all a film, my arm wrapped round the seat. I took in the scene racing towards us. The innocuous huddle of the Customs house, white with a red roof, the red-and-white bar across the road, the deserted fields smiling in the early sun; and I just had time to see that the bar would clear the bonnet of the car and no more before my head was on the seat and I was weeping with terror, and there was a shattering crash and then another second filled with the sigh of glass, which I could feel cutting my hands and neck. I raised myself from the seat. There was glass everywhere in a thick crunching pile. The air whipped through where the windscreen had been and I could feel it dragging my face into fantastic shapes. I looked at Marchmare through slitted eyes. He sat gripping the wheel, motionless. Blood ran down over the wheel and his arms in a steady stream. It seemed strange the way the car hurtled heedlessly down the very centre of the road towards the Czech post.

'Morrie!' I shouted. 'Morrie! Are you all right?'

He shouted something.

'I can't hear you!' I screamed.

I heard him this time. 'I'm blind,' he said.

'For Jesus' sake slow down! It's not worth it. Slow down.'

'*No!*' he shouted. 'Now for the Czechs!'

I saw the Czech post then. I estimated its distance at three hundred yards. There was no question of slowing down. Already it was two hundred. Three men in drab uniforms and flat hats stood their ground at the barrier. They held rifles, aimed straight at us. Before I'd registered that there was a double bang. The tyres.

Marchmare's face turned to me slowly, a mask of blood below the shapeless eyes. I saw his lips frame words. He made no attempt to deal with the car, anyway it would have been useless. I could feel it turning round and round in the road. One of the three men fired again and the bullet clanged into the engine but made no impression. There was a shriek of rubber and that smell of burning; I could hear the flap of the two punctures and the rims screaming on the asphalt. The police scattered and the car crashed sideways into the stone wall on the left of the road with a ripping of metal, and then going diagonally we hit the Customs building with the rear fender, and maybe that was what saved our lives. The three police appeared from behind the bank beyond the barrier and approached with rifles levelled from the waist. The foremost put his head cautiously inside the smoking wreck.

I peered cautiously back at him, shakily raising my hands. I felt all right except for a dizziness that threatened to swamp me and a flaming pain in my kneecap which was torture to bend. But I *could* bend it. Marchmare was laying half-sprawled on the seat, one hand still gripping the wheel. But he was moving. I don't know what kind of pain he can have been in.

'I'm all right,' he said. The three of them got us out through the window spaces. There was no glass left in the car at all. Marchmare could stand, so we stood rather helplessly in the road, the three Czech police looking at us unsmilingly out of light-blue eyes.

'Well,' I muttered to Marchmare, 'that's that.' He said nothing, appearing to stare down the road, the blood running more slowly now.

'Where's the sun, morrie?' he said at last.

'Right in front of you.'

'Okay, thanks.'

I hopped up and down on the road. It hurt me to stand still on my left leg for long. I looked back up the road and saw three more figures bicycling frantically towards us. The krauts were joining in.

The eldest of these threw himself off his bicycle purple in the face, took hold of me and started shaking me. He broke the spell. Everyone burst into torrents of Czech and German. I began to sweat cold and feel sick. Dimly I heard the bright snick of handcuffs. I forced my eyes open and found myself attached to a young German policeman. Another one approached

Marchmare, who was leaning wearily against the wall. The policeman looked at him doubtfully, while the two seniors argued; I got the impression they were fighting over who was going to have us. I was past caring who won. My eyes wandered over the car, which sagged drunkenly on its broken springs, surrounded by a litter of glass which sparkled brightly in the sun. The third German policeman was at last going up to Marchmare with a pair of handcuffs. Without giving the least warning, Marchmare began to run in the direction I had given him—to the east, into the sun. He had run about thirty yards, tripping and falling and hitting the road and recovering and going on into Czech territory before anyone recovered from their surprise. I saw the Germans struggling with their holsters and pulled desperately on my handcuffs, hearing myself shouting wordlessly. Looking at the five men, the Germans seemed reluctant to fire. Only one of them had his pistol out, the senior. But up went all the Czech rifles.

I found words. 'Morrie! Morrie!' I screamed at him. 'Stop, for Christ's sake! They're going to *shoot*!' For reply, he bent nearly double and moved like a hare with his arms spread out to fend off obstacles. Yes, I suppose he heard me but he never slowed, just started zigzagging.

The Czechs fired together, calmly.

Probably all three bullets hit him because he went over and over as if he'd been hit by a bus. With his last dive, the impetus of his running still with him, he hit the ground with his face, leaving a black smear on the cobbles. The Czechs started walking casually towards where he lay, putting their rifles under their arms and fumbling at their breast pockets for notebooks. A fly darted past me, glittering, then another. The Germans walked me up to the barrier and I could see him clearly, rolled over face upwards: his teeth, the only white thing in his face, fixed in a tight grin towards the sky, where there was nothing whatever to laugh at. I dragged my captor round towards the wall and was sick.

20

WELL, that's about it. They brought me back by air —I certainly got the veep treatment. They took me down to Rome Street nick for a kick-off. I'll say this for the Yard, they were okay about Marchmare on the whole. But Plinth was *murder*. He went on and on about him till I told the silly bastard to belt up, and he gave me a terrible wack so's I still can't hardly open my mouth. Christice and Mrs. Marengo tried to get me out on bail, the old loyals—they didn't get far with *that*, as you can imagine. Still, I was amazed them trying. No one else even wanted to know. And they've got me a super lawyer—a sharp middle-aged geezer like a cabinet minister who knows it all backwards and looks all about trout. I used to see him noshing at the Trois Assommeurs, would you believe it? So maybe he'll get a year knocked off for me.

And the *linens*! My dear, you'd have thought I'd been shot into space! They've been having a wicked time down at Tumbledown, thanks to them, of course. Press jams with the headlights on parked in the drive and all that lark. I don't know what my great-grandmother would have said, ducky, and I'll bet my old mum went nearly potty—it must have been *far* worse than the bawdy-houses. Still, it's made good reading —banners in the *Express* AND the *Mail*. I shouldn't wonder if Flook had a go at it.

And it's not over yet. Here I am at Brixton waiting for my daily visit from the law in that little granite room I mentioned somewhere. 'Course they got me remanded at the magistrates' court (and boy was it *packed*), so it's still only the beginning. And every reporter on the Street's weeping with joy over it. I wish I was doing the same.

Oh, well . . . that's how it happens. I reckon myself I'll be going down for a five less the remission, and I know I'm still in for a beating or two when I don't grass. Same for the Archbubble. (He's here, too, setting up a right scream three cells away.) Well, then they'll get to the silly trial in the death and reach their old verdict, which they'll publish with the judge's crusty remarks for everyone to yawp over in the linens. And come to a rub it'll be nishte because I'm not trying to save myself, so in the death everyone'll be happy—me because I haven't grassed anyone and the law because they can write closed on the file . . . just honour satisfied with the taxpayer footing the jack-and-jill. It's a funny affair, this justice biz, the closer you are to it, the dodgier it looks. To tell the truth, though, all this bit's an anticlimax after what I've been through. That time waiting to do the frontier I thought I'd be topped for sure, not to mention the spandau at Kassburg. All in all, Marchmare's the thing I'm really choked over—he was dead loyal, wasn't he? and he had what it takes, say what you like.

Well, so I'll go into the nick, won't I? with a right fat property and read a lot of books—something I've never had a chance to do since I left school—and be a snout-baron. I'm the philosophical type when it comes to it, as you have to be or else crack up. Oh, the screws'll probably pee over my cell for a day or two at first, just for the hell of it, anyway they ease off in the death, the way people do if you give them time. So I'll sit in my cell reading and laugh about Geneva and think of all that loot waiting for the Archbubble and me when we get out . . . time'll pass the way it does if you leave it alone. Very likely I'll take up Zen in there and learn to clap with one hand and all that crap, and puzzle the screws by standing on my head. *And* I'll earn my remission like a good little boy.

It could've been a lot worse, couldn't it?

And then one day I'll be out, and that day I'll be back in biz with the Archbubble with fifteen grand all of my very own. Maybe I'll buy a ranch in the Argentine, or else a big red motor and go off looking for tourist bird and graft along the bright spring banks of the Seine—after all, five years isn't for ever.

Founded in 1986, Serpent's Tail publishes the innovative and the challenging.

If you would like to receive a catalogue of our current publications please write to:

FREEPOST
Serpent's Tail
4 Blackstock Mews
LONDON N4 2BR

(No stamp necessary if your letter is posted in the United Kingdom.)

Murder in the Central Committee

The Angst-Ridden Executive

An Olympic Death

Southern Seas

Pepe Carvalho thrillers by

Manuel Vazquez Montalban

Murder in Memoriam
Didier Daeninckx

"Didier Daeninckx is a novelist, magician and archeologist prince. He unlimbs French moral and political life in *Murder in Memoriam*. His hero, Inspector Cadin, is both catalyst and seer into the past: the crime he solves is nothing less than the 'trick' of an entire culture to create its own selective amnesia . . . Daeninckx has written a frightening book."
JEROME CHARYN

"Captures the smell of cowardly assassination carried out for the basest of all motives, extremism revealed as self-interest, political corruption, and the stoking of racial prejudice to achieve political ends . . . *Murder in Memoriam* serves as a tap on the shoulder — a necessary reminder that what is dead is not buried, and what is buried is, unfortunately, not dead."
DEREK RAYMOND

Devil in a Blue Dress
Walter Mosley

"A magnificent first novel by Walter Mosley in which, from the first page, it's clear we have discovered a wonderful new talent . . . the most exciting arrival in the genre for years."

Financial Times

"A first novel of astonishing virtuosity, upending Chandler's LA to show a dark side of a different kind." *Sunday Times*

"A brilliant novel. Period. Mosley's prose is rich, yet taut, and has that special musical cadence that few writers achieve . . . I read *Devil in a Blue Dress* in one sitting and didn't want it to end. An astonishing first novel." JONATHAN KELLERMAN

"A fresh new voice, a riveting story and a protagonist who'll stay with you awhile. Welcome Ezekiel Rawlins, black P.I., who – if the breaks go Mosley's way – just might be the stuff of classics."

Philadelphia Inquirer

"Mosley has given American crime fiction another unique hero and a solid mystery, all the way to the brilliant, existential last page."

San Francisco Chronicle

"Marks the debut of a talented author with something vital to say about the distance between the black and white worlds, and a dramatic way to say it. Easy and Mouse are a team who deserve to be heard from again." *New York Times*

"A black Chinatown, a cross between Richard Wright and Raymond Chandler." *New York*

A Red Death
Walter Mosley

"Confirms the advent of an extraordinary storyteller
... Mosley with his unique talents, may well be in the
process of creating a genre classic."

Publishers Weekly

"The fascinating and vividly rendered world of Easy
Rawlins seems at once exotic and believable, filled
with memorable individuals and morally complex
situations." *Wall Street Journal*

"Walter Mosley has depicted a special locale and a
corner-cutting way of life that most readers will find
far more riveting than the crime pages of their
newspapers." *New York Times*

"Readers, be warned – this is about as far as you can
get from the cozy English mystery. The idiom is
harsh, syncopated, sometimes downbeat, but always
exhilaratingly tender." *Philadelphia Inquirer*

I, Anna
Elsa Lewin

"Marriage, divorce, sexual animosity and isolation are the subjects of this fascinating, psychological suspense story."   *Library Journal*

"A brilliant character study of a middle-aged woman who has lost her husband to a younger woman and her daughter to maturity."   *Booklist*

"Freud would have loved this passion-hate tale of a desperate woman, a lonely detective, and a victim who demanded more than Anna could offer."

LUCY FREEMAN

"A shocking, bleak but poetic psychological thriller that makes *Fatal Attraction* seem like a bloodless coup."   *Time Out*

A Long Cold Fall
Sam Reaves

"Sam Reaves is too good, he makes me nervous. *A Long Cold Fall* is as hard and muscular as the early Hammett, and as full of promise."

ROBERT B. PARKER

"An exemplary beginning. The setting is Chicago, whose infinite and frequent acrid variety Reaves appears to know as well as does Sara Paretsky."

Los Angeles Times

"This impressive debut grabs attention with its opening chapter and never lets up."

Publishers Weekly